I0745760

STARS IN OUR EYES

twenty stories

W. M. Raebeck

Hula
Cat
Press

in lasting, loving memory of Leslie Raebeck

~ warrior, singer/songwriter, trailblazer ~
always an original
the gutsiest of all

I hear your giggle, Les.

ACKNOWLEDGEMENTS

A special thanks to Donna Carsten for her corrections and editorial help in the final drafts of this book. And gratitude goes to Marcie Powers, for her preliminary read-through and encouragement back when this book had only six stories.

I also want to thank Gillian Gordon for luring me to L.A. and for always being all heart.

*

This is a book about artists, friends, family, and spirits — all who I thank for the inspiration, loyalty, support, and fun. It seemed so risky all those years back to not be normal, to stay up all night printing photos in the darkroom or sitting at the typewriter. As a religion, really. This book is in honor of the "raw space" in downtown Manhattan — as we once called the manufacturing lofts we all converted to living quarters. This is in memory of all that under-heated, industrial square footage where creatives found a totally new way to live in the City. In those rough lofts, we made something out of nothing. And our art was the same. We lived with art, slept in it, woke up to it, our lives were devoted to *making something* out of nothing.

And even though we were warned and scorned and fraught with anxiety, we had each other and our visions. And we endured. I never would have believed in 1972 in

North London or 1974 in New York, when Tribeca wasn't even named yet, that an artsy band of international outliers bonded by a commitment to never giving up, would actually do well in life. I never imagined that in 2017, we'd be on the other end of that determination and tenacity, and still know each other, still be making art, still be laughing, and…have fared surprisingly well. We were expected to surrender, not thrive.

Years ago, when I was wondering about the exit door, I asked my dear and wizened friend Robert Janz—who, at age 86, is still doing street art in Downtown New York—"Bob, is there such a thing as an ex-artist?"

"Unfortunately, no," he answered.

to

The Artistes

TABLE OF CONTENTS

If you can't be good, be good material.

THE GHOST OF BRIAN JONES

Since he was a ghost, there's no point in wondering where is he now. He's around.

Meeting Brian wasn't a tale I often told. As a ghost story, there were too many knowns; as a straight road story, too many unknowns. In fact, he only ever came up in reminiscences with Michael, who, thankfully, was with me at the time.

It was August 1980. Michael and I were on our second weekend trip south of the border together, which he still insists was our first. In remembering Brian, however, our recollections are alike. We were heading south from Ensenada in 'Death Car,' a fine green Mercedes that earned its name on that journey (from the Brian episode among others). Since we both subscribed to the adage, "Getting there is ALL the fun," and since the only choice offered the Baja traveler is north or south—the eight hundred-mile peninsula is so slim—we were essentially just watching a plotless movie, 'Cactus,' playing in all the windows. Michael had his surfboard on the roof, in hopes of sharpening his technique before placing his ad in the LA Weekly personals: "Aging agent with surfboard seeks same." And on the arid August road, piercing endless miles of scorched nothing, we were as foolish as we were jubilant, and the only car out there.

It was our second day, mid-afternoon, and too hot to even get out of the car. Cruising at an air-conditioned sixty, we rounded a lazy bend to see a hitch-hiker on the shoulder ahead. To pass him would've been manslaughter, so we didn't.

But as our grateful new companion climbed into the back seat, dubious looks filled the front. This small, spare-framed soul in unkempt denim carried nothing but a folded blanket, and wore across his forehead layers of caked scabs. Michael shot me an against-my-better-judgment look before lifting his foot from the brake. But we could fend off the hitcher better than he could fend off the desert, so I nodded past Michael's look and we eased back onto the road. Cruising now at an apprehensive thirty, I was turned in my seat, eyes trained on our passenger. No way would we turn our backs on this nut, and Michael was restricted to driving. As I imagined our carcasses roasting with the cacti while the car, surfboard, and battered stranger continued south, Michael slid his hand into the pocket of his door where he kept his knife.

"I really appreciate this," said the rider, with no false earnestness.

"What were you doing out there?" Michael asked.

"I was dropped off here," answered the scrawny guy.

"By your last ride? They must've liked you."

"No, they didn't like me."

We continued along the isolated pavement, me twisted unnaturally in my seat, eyes glued on the man, and Michael asking himself almost audibly whether or not to unload this cargo right there.

"Is that all you're traveling with?" I asked, shifting my focus to the blanket, perfect size for concealing a weapon.

"Yeah," he shrugged.

"You're American, aren't you?" said Michael. "Where you comin' from?"

"San Francisco."

Michael and I looked at each other. San Francisco was a thousand miles north. The man said nothing more.

"When did you leave there?" I pressed.

"Two days ago."

"Where you headed?"

"Cabo."

"Cabo?" Michael stopped the car completely to turn and study the man. "You're hitching from San Francisco to Cabo with just a blanket? You're out of your mind, aren't you? You're a loony."

"I started out with a couple of bags," said the little guy, "but I had some trouble."

"Looks like it," said Michael. "What happened to your head?"

"This is from the sun," he rubbed the bloody scabs. "They keep peeling then getting sunburned again. I lost my hat with the rest of my stuff."

"What happened?" I asked, as Death Car patiently idled.

"Well, when I got to Tijuana it was night. So I went in this bar. I met some local guys and asked if they knew where I could score some amphetamines—"

"Amphetamines?" Michael cut in.

"Yeah."

"Oh great, that's terrific. Go on."

"They took me to this place, but then they rolled me and took all my money."

"Why didn't you just hitch back to San Francisco?" Michael wanted to know. "You'll never make it to Cabo with no money. And if somehow you do, you'll never get back. I mean we're only going about another hour, then you're back out in the desert."

"Why are you going down there in the first place?" I asked.

"I was gonna sell the amphetamines down in Cabo then

buy some speed to bring back up to Frisco. I heard they have good stuff down there. And cheap."

"You are a loony," said Michael. "You can't buy it without any money."

"I know, but since I got this far I figured I should keep going."

"With nothing at all and not a penny?!" Michael gave a hoot.

"I still had my bags," said the stranger. "They didn't take my stuff, just my money."

"Where's your stuff then?" I asked.

"My next ride took it."

"You're 0 for 2," said Michael. "I guess you expect us to grab the blanket. This all sounds a little pathetic, you know."

"Yeah," said the man, smiling sweetly.

"So?" probed Michael, returning his foot to the gas pedal. He'd now removed his hand from the door pocket, knifeless, apparently deciding our passenger was more suicidal than homicidal.

"Oh," said the man, "...so the next morning, a truckful of Mexicans picked me up and said they'd take me to Ensenada. Once we got to Ensenada, they said I should hang around and eat with them and stuff, so I did. But that night, we all got real drunk. We were sittin' around this fire outside somewhere—I don't know where we were—and they turned on me and said they wanted all my money. I told them I didn't have any, but they didn't believe me, so they took all my stuff and left. They threw me this blanket so I wouldn't freeze. I must've passed out after that.... Then today you two came along. And I'm very appreciative, I want you to know."

We rode in silence for a while, passing fifty-foot cacti on both sides.

"What's your name?" I asked, after a time.

"Brian Jones."

"Brian Jones of The Rolling Stones?" Michael chuckled.

"Yes," said the passenger.

"Brian Jones is DEAD," Michael said firmly, his voice warning the rider not to push his credibility another hair.

"Well…" Brian started, glancing from my face over to Michael's in the rearview mirror, and back a few times, "it all began on July third, 1969."

"Oh no," I muttered.

Michael looked at me, "What?"

"July third's my birthday," I said, with some resignation. I'd always found coincidence a key ingredient in spiritual matters—now here it was again. "Go on, Brian." I nestled against my door. Maybe there was more to this seemingly inconsequential being than met the eye. He'd already succeeded in the near-impossible twice in just fifteen minutes—first in getting a ride where none was to be had, and now in capturing himself one hundred per cent of the available audience in this Baja wasteland.

The desertscape consumed us again and Brian's childlike voice became a soundtrack. "I was out by the pool at a party in San Francisco. I had dropped six thousand mics of acid, so I was affected by what happened even more than I otherwise might have been."

"Six thousand mics!" Michael shouted. "What's that, two hundred tabs?"

"I'm not exactly sure," said Brian. "Anyway, somebody at the party came outside and announced that the radio had just said Brian Jones had died in England. That he drowned. And there I was sitting right by a pool. Everybody was shocked and upset, but right at that moment I felt a kind of haze come over me. I seemed to rise up above the party, everything was kind of foggy, and I could see everyone below milling around and talking about Brian Jones and how awful it was. It seemed almost as if I was dying, too. I'm still not sure whether I died or not."

"Six thousand micrograms? Good chance you did," offered Michael.

"Yeah," said Brian. "Anyway, I was feeling very strange, not like myself. And I felt Brian Jones enter into my body. I knew it was him. I could tell because I immediately felt okay about his death. I knew he was back and that he wanted me to help him. Like he wanted to live in my body. And I realized that he was important to the world and that I should help him. I wouldn't be sacrificing anything really because I wasn't doing much anyway. And since that day, I became him. More and more. I mean there's this thing that started happening that makes it impossible not to believe I'm him: sometimes I can pick up a guitar and play incredible licks, and I've never studied guitar. I never played in my life till after that day by the pool. And now, when other people hear me play—when it just comes to me and I start playing— they think it's great music. And it's exactly the music Brian would've played. I try not to tell people about all this unless they ask me about my name. But since you asked, and since we have a little time, I thought I should tell you the truth."

"So why don't you join The Rolling Stones?" Michael suggested. "You could make some money. Though, I have to say, you don't look much like him."

"Not right now," said Brian, "but I look exactly like him when I wear clothes like his and a long blond wig. Then I look like him in a way that's, well, unbelievable."

"Do that often?" Michael exchanged an eye-roll with me.

"Only when I'm playing music or something, then it's important to look right. And when I went to see Mick Jagger, I wore the wig and the clothes to make sure Mick knew I really was Brian."

The story went on with our new acquaintance obtaining Jagger's address, thumbing to New York, then flying to London (or traveling through the slipstream) to present himself at Jagger's door, dressed as Brian Jones, complete with platinum tresses.

He rang the bell.

"Mick's not in," said a voice through the intercom.

"When will he be back?"

"Who is it who would like to know?"

"Brian Jones. It's important that I see him."

"Important indeed," agreed the voice. "He'll be back in a few hours."

"Thank you. I'll come back later."

Returning in the afternoon, Brian rang the bell and announced himself again. In moments, the door was opened by Mick himself.

"Hi," said Brian, stepping back to allow Mick the full impact. (Or 'surprise,' as Brian put it.)

"Hi," said Mick. And they studied each other in silence, equally awestruck and uncertain about what would happen next.

"Well, I'm here," said Brian finally.

"I see," said Mick.

"What should I do?" asked Brian, after a beat.

"What....would.....you.....like to do?" asked Mick slowly.

"I'd like to do whatever's best for the group," answered Brian.

Mick thought it over and then told Brian he thought the best thing would be for Brian to go back to New York. Right away. And he offered to pay for the ticket.

Brian respected Mick's decision that New York was where he should go; Mick knew best about things Rolling Stone. And he was honored that Mick was popping for the fare. It meant he understood. "Is New York where you think I can be most effective?" he double-checked.

"Yes," said Mick, with a reassuring certainty.

And the next day, Brian flew out.

By the end of Brian's narration, Michael and I had been lulled out of our earlier assessments. Brian's innocence was as compelling as his unorthodox travel style. Besides, making character judgments about spirits or penniless hitch-hikers in the midday summer desert would make us the weird ones, so why bother? (The surfboard on the roof in the middle of the desert had already been questioned even by the all-accepting Brian.) And the stark panorama—we were now engulfed by a valley of treelike, black cacti, looming, and eerie—produced an increasing awareness that we three were lone travelers on the lengthy peninsula. And Brian was therefore not only like us, despite his claim, but vital. And, as we clocked up a half hour in his company, he grew even likable.

Around this time, we spotted some irresistible rock formations. "Hey Brian," said Michael, "would you mind a divergence from the Cabo trail? Or is your schedule too tight?"

With his eager nod, Brian scored another niceness point, and the three of us left the vehicle and climbed onto the sprawling round red rocks.

Michael stayed below to examine some religious graffiti painted on the lower stones in Mexican yellows, aquas, and reds, while Brian and I climbed to the top. With our feet on the rocks and our eyes in the sky, little Bri seemed peaceful if not indigenous. Sitting together on an upper perch, we shared a grapefruit and enjoyed the quiet. The distinctions of who, what, where, and why dissolved before the magnificence of the expansive, cactus-speckled desert below, and we now were not different but quite alike in our isolated humanness out here. This wavering spirit by my side was gentle, congenial, and just the sort you'd wish to occupy a desert boulder with. Maybe people with nothing are easy to please, maybe Brian was just cool; either way, we rejoined Michael as friends.

As the three of us lingered in the shade of the mighty stones, our contented mood absorbed Michael, too. And rolling along again soon after, our feelings for Brian were transforming from distrustful condescension to genuine concern. Earlier we'd been worried about ourselves, now we were worried about him.

We drove along without talking. Brian gazed pleasantly out the window as Michael and I both considered the moral and physical ramifications of what we'd soon do: leave Brian to his fate as we checked into the El Presidente Hotel in Cataviña, where we'd be spending the night. The town beyond that was hundreds of miles away.

Should we keep Brian with us? Three in a room? A room of his own? Then what about tomorrow? We'd be turning off to the east toward the Gulf of Mexico, then the following day zooming all the way back to LA. Brian was en route to Cabo San Lucas, Baja's southern-most tip, seven hundred miles south. At some point, we had to return him to his life-or-death struggle with the searing road. Should we give him money—just to have it stolen or to buy drugs with? Or should we take him at face value, leave him to his ghostness, and let him follow the course he was so uniquely on? As far as faith went, he was clearly well-endowed; there was no other way he could have embarked on a journey that void of possibility.

"Hey Bri, what're you gonna do when we get to Cataviña?" asked Michael.

"Just keep hitching, I guess," said Brian with an implike smile, benignly accepting his fate.

"But it's almost four o'clock," I said. "Where're you gonna sleep tonight?"

"I don't know," said Brian. "I'll just see what happens."

"But there are no cars," said Michael and I together.

"Oh well," said Brian.

As we rounded a curve, the cubic whiteness of the Cataviña El Presidente jumped into our vista like a set of desert teeth. In moments, we were pulling in beside the seven or eight jeeps and campers already stationed in the parking lot, and knowing anyone on the road behind us would be arriving shortly. Nobody navigates Baja by night.

There was an unhappy moment as Michael, Brian, and I got out of the car, a cruel hit-and-run aspect to letting anyone, mortal or im-, do what Brian was about to. But in this last chance to alter his future, by adopting him for a night or a week, there seemed an equal futility in investing in an illusion, trying to give substance to that which epitomized the invisible.

So we gave Brian a few bucks and the last grapefruit, and just said good luck. The amount of luck he needed, though, didn't exist, and we all had to smile at the emptiness of the two words.

As we took our things from the trunk and walked to the hotel entrance, we watched Brian's slight denim figure amble out to the vacant road. And though we wondered about him aloud inside the hotel, and voiced thoughts we'd each had before setting him free, we kept returning to the notion of Brian's reality or non-reality being very much his, and to the uselessness of tampering with that kind of karma or plight. After an hour, we looked out the front entrance and up the road. Brian had disappeared.

Or we thought he disappeared. Curiously, though, his presence seemed to grow as time passed. We continued to talk about him and ponder his lonely quest. On the road next morning, we rounded each turn with hopes of spotting his vertical blue form, and fears of finding him horizontal instead — the latter overwhelming us with guilt, the former offering us a second chance.

We wouldn't know what to do with him, of course, but whole-heartedly agreed, not knowing quite why, that if he reappeared we would take greater responsibility, even if it meant driving to Cabo, God forbid, or shipping him parcel post back to San Francisco. "Bri" became a kind of punch-line for our jokes as we churned along the hot strip of pavement, but we sent out our sincerest wishes to him wherever he was. Or was he still sitting in the back seat?

By the time we got back to LA, the powerless vagabond had become the essence of our journey. But more the strange moral quandary he'd represented, more the spirit of the man, than the meager skeleton we'd transported, bonded Michael and me on some outer plane. Was he real, or a ghost who'd placed himself in our path? Why did his commitment to nothingness and his dependence on faith make us awkward and unsure?

Not long ago, while talking with Blake—a friend who used to spend time in LA with Rolling Stone Ron Wood—the name Brian Jones came up, and I had to smile.

"Why are you smiling like that?" asked Blake.

"Oh…I once had an encounter with someone who claimed to be the ghost of Brian Jones."

"You did?" Blake's interest sharpened. "Did he look like Brian Jones?"

"No. Just like a scraggly guy. But he apparently had a disguise he could effect, wig and all, when the mood struck. That's what he told me and my friend, anyway, and for some reason we believed him."

"Know what," said Blake, "I think I met the same guy. It was a long time ago, though, like back in 1980. I was over at Wood's house one day and a guy dressed up as Brian Jones knocked on the door.

"Wood wasn't expecting any visitors that day, and he lived way up in a canyon on this little road that was hard to find or get to, and suddenly there was a knock on the door. When Wood answered it, there was this weird guy standing there with shoulder-length blond hair, saying he was Brian Jones. The disguise wasn't very good, not to mention the fact that Jones was dead. I mean, the wig was ridiculous, and the whole picture was pretty odd. Wood, of course, didn't have any idea what to do with the guy… because the guy was so into it, and so…unassuming."

"That's Bri, that's our boy!" I was warmed all over by this belated evidence that he'd not only told us the truth, but apparently survived Baja.

"He was easy-going enough," Blake went on, "but nobody knew what the hell to do with him. And after a while it grew pretty clear that he just couldn't stick around. So Wood told him it was time to go. Who knows how he got there or where he went."

"Who knows?" I echoed.

Finishing this story in November 1987, I wanted to check that the original Brian Jones spelled his name with an `i,' so I dialed the number of another friend, also named Michael, this one a musician.

"Hello?" a male voice answered.

"You don't sound like Michael," I said.

"I'm not," answered the voice. "Wanna speak to him?"

"Please. Tell him I've got a rock 'n' roll trivia question."

"What's up?" This voice was Michael's.

"Is Brian Jones spelled with an `i' or a `y'?"

"Which one?" asked Michael.

"Why? How many do you know?" I laughed.

"Well, there's Brian Jones from The Rolling Stones, spelled with an `i,' and there's my buddy, Bryan Jones, spelled with a `y.'"

"Oh," I said. "Well, thanks. It was the Stones one I wondered about.... You also have a friend named Bryan Jones?"

"Yeah," said Michael, "a carpenter friend of mine. Known him for years. He's here right now — that's who answered the phone."

What are the chances someone named Bryan Jones would answer the phone when I called a friend to ask the spelling of that precise name? But I'd always found coincidence a key ingredient in spiritual matters.

✳ ✳ ✳

THE ROUND TABLE

I was at the age where you keep nothing from your best friend and everything from your parents—a teenager. Being slighted was a daily diet. That, and not measuring up physically. That, and reasonable certainty that the crush on the sporty upper classman wasn't ever going to pan out.

High school was hardly exciting or romantic. Especially compared to a book like 'Gone With the Wind.' And being young was even something of a curse, with your imagination luring you over distant horizons while in reality you climbed on and off the school bus every day.

Music helped a little. We had The Beatles. They were real, at least, though not exactly accessible.

The fact was, no one was accessible when it came to true love—because we were too young; we had to wait.

But wait till when? How do you know when your time has come?

"It just happens...you'll know. But not yet, you're too young."

In many households in 1967, listening to albums of Broadway musicals was a favorite pastime. We kids would read the play's synopsis on the record jacket, then learn the songs, and eventually perform the entire show for our parents and their friends from New York City. Martinis in hand, they enjoyed nothing more than our robust renditions of My Fair Lady, Camelot, Oliver, West Side Story, and the rest. And we adored belting out the struggles, love, and longing of kings, queens, swindlers, paupers, and princes.

On Easter break, when I was sixteen, the whole family took a road trip from Long Island to Miami. We were all craving some sun and salt water. So we sang our way to Florida, two or three long days in the car, interspersed with Howard Johnson's restaurants and motels.

'Camelot' was made into a movie that year, hardly a production a tribe like mine would pass up. Especially since my father had something of a King Arthur complex, seemed emotionally entwined with the Camelot legend, and referred to it wistfully when everyone else was in the present moment. Thus, while in Miami, we were all up for seeing the new Camelot movie. As New Yorkers, the film versions of our shows always seemed lesser imitations, but on vacation this outing would be the perfect treat. And, for the only time in our family history, all eight of us went to the cinema together.

As everyone knows, the story of King Arthur, Guinevere, and Sir Lancelot is compelling — not to mention the brilliant music and lyrics familiar to one and all. And for a sixteen-year-old girl, already stoned on Florida's balmy breezes, the romance between Sir Lancelot and Queen Guinevere was practically medicinal. With King Arthur so good and well-intentioned, Guinevere's conflict was somehow everybody's: what do you do about passionate love that arrives at the wrong time?

Rhett and Scarlett had only been in a book, but these two were now right before my eyes, larger than life. And there was additional sizzle — the actor who played Lancelot was unbearably handsome. Anyone watching this picture knew that no Guinevere — not Vanessa Redgrave, Julie Andrews, or any other actress or princess — could resist this Knight of the Round Table. (Sorry, King Arthur.)

So I'm watching the movie…and I mean Broadway's Robert Goulet had done a bang-up job, but suddenly here comes this whole new Lancelot, bronzed and square-shouldered, coat of mail and ocean eyes gleaming in the sun, literally arriving on a prancing steed.

And I'm sweet sixteen, I don't stand a chance.

And this actor was a real person — he was alive somewhere.

I guess it's commonplace to be smitten by movie stars. I now comprehended how it happens. I would definitely take note of this actor's name and watch for him in future films.

So, as the others readied to leave after the movie, I had to linger. "Come on," they said.

"I'm coming, I'm coming…." I edged backwards out of the theater, unwilling to explain my sudden interest in film credits.

Fortunately, the actor's name popped up quickly: Franco Nero. I'd never heard of him. In 1967, this was clearly a foreign name. Who was he? Would I see him in other movies? Did he live in another country? I memorized the name, should I ever have the chance to watch him again.

But it didn't happen.

Many years later (though now fourteen doesn't seem so many at all), I was now a film and television actress myself, living and working in London. I'd had passions of my own by then, as well as pain. In fact, on this very occasion, I was putting the brakes on a troubled love affair.

I had just completed the shooting of a BBC movie and was in between jobs. Winter was bleak, and I decided to take a breather and visit a girlfriend in Rome.

Meanwhile, an older Italian producer had invited me to lunch on this particular London day. Contacts like producers and directors are taken quite seriously by film actresses. You pretend it's all business and camaraderie, yet everyone knows who wants what from whom. I was safe with Fernando, though, who had become a friend. He knew I lived with my English boyfriend. Fernando would simply phone when he was in town and we'd meet sometimes for lunch. A producer of note, he wasn't a bad connection (though he worked mainly in Italy), and was always the gentleman.

Meeting that day, he asked why I'd brought my suitcase.

"I'm going to Rome right after lunch," I said.

"Oh, me, too. We go togedder!"

"I don't think so," I said, "I'm hitching."

Fernando, someone with gray hair turning white, didn't like this idea. "I tell you what," he said, "we go to the Playboy Club for lunch. They have a casino there and I try to win some money. If I win, I buy you a plane ticket and you fly with me."

"Really?"

"Sure, let's go."

As it happened, he won. So after lunch, we went to the airport and flew to Rome togedder. And though my Italian girlfriend wouldn't be back in town for another day, Fernando assured me not to worry about where to stay, he had lots of friends.

I was glad he'd mentioned that when I saw that his own apartment was a one-bedroom. He traveled so much that was all he needed, he said. "And don't worry," he reassured me, "I make a phone call and you have a good place to sleep tonight." And he did just that as I grabbed a shower and change of clothes before dinner. "Take your suitcase wid us to the restaurant," he said, "because you go to my friend's house after dinner."

The Italian film business, it turned out, was miniscule compared to LA, New York, and London. And Fernando was a senior player in a circle of filmmakers who'd worked together for years. Food being a huge factor in Mediterranean life, the custom was for these Romans to gather late at night in any one of the city's elegant eateries, and to dine, drink, laugh, and talk shop into the early morning hours.

That first night, we didn't even set out for dinner until after 10. And upon arrival at the architectural masterpiece of a restaurant, we were led to a long table of ten or twelve people—all Fernando's associates and all partway into a meal that seemed short on structure and long on tempting plates of food passed generously to and fro.

I was tired, whipped by hurtin' love (but proud to have bolted it), and generally taken by the Italian splendor. I couldn't have found a better escort than Fernando, who now introduced me to his gang. I wasn't polished on my Italian film credits, but was meeting key players in the industry (though Federico Fellini, Lina Wertmüller, and Giancarlo Giannini must've been on location). The amazing food and trying to follow the animated conversation commanded my full attention, as newcomers to the repast floated in. Fernando warmly introduced me to each one. Then, amidst the din of forks and sing-song Italian, he leaned over to me. "Do you know Franco?" he asked quietly, indicating the man across the table.

"No, I don't."

"You don't know Franco Nero? He's a big actor in England and the U.S."

"Oh-h, Franco Nero?" Were my ears deceiving me? "Uh, yes, I do know who he is."

"He's the friend I just introduced you to. You're going to stay at his house tonight."

"I am?"

"Yes. Is that okay?"

"Um, sure…if he's your friend…. Does he know you want me to stay there tonight?"

"Yes, I called and asked him earlier. He said you are welcome."

Well, I'd gotten over Sir Lancelot a while back, but hadn't forgotten the name or how entranced I'd been. I hadn't seen or heard of him since watching Camelot that night in Miami, though obviously his career had gone swimmingly. "He was married to Vanessa Redgrave," Fernando now imparted. "They are divorced, but they have a son togedder."

I surreptitiously studied my soon-to-be host, instantly wishing at least ten of the fourteen years hadn't passed. And wishing, too, that I wasn't so stuck on this difficult Englishman right now. Still, Franco Nero, right across the table?

I smiled and made it known to him that I was a friendly foreigner, despite knowing no Italian. He was friendly, too, but not nearly as handy with English as one might have expected from a knight of Camelot.

My prevailing feeling was awe — awe at how life works. And I could only imagine my total disbelief if some time traveler had whispered in my ear during that screening of Camelot, "You're going to meet him, and you're going to spend the night in his house in Italy."

Right.

So the dinner wound down. It was 1 a.m. Fernando went one way, while Franco and I drove off the other.

I have to say that at age twenty-nine, almost thirty, I was not only in love with someone else, but also a bit picky in what I sought in a mate. Though still a specimen, not to mention a celebrity and Knight of the Round Table, Franco, it pains me to say, really wasn't my type. It must sound weird, but he had a certain Italian smoothness maybe a tad slick for my earthy tastes — was his car too new, maybe the shoes were wrong? I can't pinpoint the minutia. Still, as we drove toward the outskirts of Rome and up a hill, I remained somewhat breathless at being driven anywhere by Franco Nero, least of all to his home in Rome to sleep over. Just the two of us. I glanced in his direction once or twice for verification. He had matured, but was definitely that extremely handsome and gallant guy from the movie.

In his home, Franco was remarkably polite. Since it was so late and we were satiated by the six- or seven-course meal, he sweetly showed me his home, framed photos of Vanessa and his son, and then the guest room and guest bathroom, that had clearly been readied for a visitor. Surprising me somewhat, he then said goodnight and that he'd make me breakfast in the morning.

I was actually impressed that there was no innuendo. I would've probably been as conflicted as Guinevere, because on the one hand I was hooked on someone else, on the other he was friggin' Sir Lancelot. From my childhood fantasy. I mean, really I should fall in love with him right now, marry, and live happily ever after. (My father would certainly approve of this courtly gent.) Plus he was single. And nice.

And was going to make me breakfast tomorrow morning.

I decided to see what the morning delivered. Maybe I'd wake up in Camelot. Maybe Richard Burton would show up. Maybe Merlin.

We both slept late, and convened in the kitchen where a sunny terra-cotta garden overlooked the City of Rome. This should be extremely romantic.

Franco was whipping up some eggs and toast, coffee was brewing. He wouldn't let me assist, needing to be the perfect host.

And he was. But he wasn't flirting with me, nor I with him. I sensed that he probably thought I was `Fernando's' (and that maybe even Fernando thought I was now Fernando's). And moreover, I knew, the way you just know things, that this wasn't the man for me.

But I absolutely loved how life plunks things like Lancelots down in your path. And that the ends to some stories don't come for years and years. And the ends to the best ones are never what you'd think.

The end to this one was a lovely breakfast at a round table with a lovely man on a scenic Italian terrace, and knowing in my heart that it was so much more than that.

✳ ✳ ✳

THE LEATHER BAG

As a child, all I wanted to do in life was travel the world. At seven, I begged for a globe for Christmas, and got one. Though there was only so much spinning of it and tripping out one could do, my planet became familiar, as did my oceans, continents, and hemispheres. I wanted to go everywhere, and now I could study where everywhere was.

And once I spread my wings, I'd occasionally meet real travelers out on the trail. They were always alone, had sturdy bags, often of leather, that were never too heavy to carry a mile or two. These folks, primarily men, weren't shabby or broke or dirty, just out seeing the world. Usually they were rugged, and generally strong, as they had to be. They had been to faraway lands I'd hardly heard of. They weren't limited by their nationality, knew languages, and were at home on the road. They'd talk of not-to-be-missed rail journeys through countries I hadn't considered, islands no one knew about, cool deals and prices. Best of all, they'd tell you their stories. Not because they were storytellers, but because everything about them was a story. Sometimes they hadn't been home in years. Home wasn't a pull for them, the world was. Travel was their life. And it was the life I wanted.

In observing these wayfarers, it seemed a strong leather bag was part of the portrait. And I learned why when I began traveling a lot. Everything but leather gives out in a year or two. And broken straps or bags with holes are the enemy of the rough and ready. (Think car with blown-out tire.) Granted, leather bags were expensive, but the best investment a tough traveler could make. So, at twenty-three, I bought myself a beauty on Fifth Avenue in NYC. Though pricey ($50), I knew I'd carry it everywhere. And that beloved bag proved the most useful accessory I've ever purchased.

I'd always lived within my means. And there was an art and skill to being a seasoned traveler. But suddenly, in the 1980's, everyone got credit cards. With plastic as the new enabler, status and appearance began to overshadow the authenticity and street smarts that had formerly been measures of maturity. Previously, what you were, what you'd learned, where you'd been, and how you inspired or were inspired, mattered more than what you had. But this new way of life was about what you drove, what you spent, where you dined, and what you had to show. For me, it wasn't unlike waking from a long, soulful dream.

At thirty-six, after laborious overtime, I had just completed the final round with that English lover. There was no one to blame. Love for its own sake guarantees no emotional or financial reward. So, upon my return to the US, I sought the safe haven of my Long Island clan, as my English reality dissolved. But in the dead of winter, I was met with shallow tolerance, even evidence that collapse threatened others' agendas, too, only they were handling it and so should I.

Okay, then I'd need to borrow some money.

My sister agreed that being a woman had never gotten us far with Dad, but I had to appeal to him. Without tears of proof—men don't have to cry for a loan, why should women?—I'd simply explain I was skint. But biting my bottom lip, the tears rolled down anyway as I listened over the phone to Dad's reasons why he couldn't help me out. "I'd have to sell some stock...." he faltered. "And I couldn't go into my retirement account."

"It's okay, Dad," I forced my voice steady. "I'll work something out."

"I mean, I could possibly give you something out of pocket," he paused, "maybe fifty or sixty bucks."

"Well, actually," I abandoned all pride, "anything would help." Painful to utter, the words cracked out of my mouth like shards of glass.

But when he and my step-mother drove me to the train station that afternoon, talking about their spiritual awakening the whole hour-ride, I had to ask how we can believe in both prosperity and `giving everything,' when one is about holding and the other about letting go. (A recent three months in Nicaragua during the Contra War had magnified this contradiction to convincing proportions.) Only in America is materialism exalted above all else.

When Dad dropped me at the station, he commented on the immensity of my load, but didn't bring up the loan again or give me anything out of pocket. He had things to do, and didn't wait with me for the train, even though I was heading to LA and wouldn't be back soon. But I felt his after-thoughts hanging in the icy air after our casual goodbye. As I turned away from his departing car to face the tracks, dragging onto the platform what felt more like a body than the winter clothes I had just retrieved from London, I said quietly to the freezing air, "You just don't get it, Dad." And I'll always remember the white steam from my breath hanging there then vanishing, just like Dad.

I felt alienated and forsaken on the train. Dad had been the last resort. I had no idea now where I'd get assistance.

And that day, for the first time, I finally understood all the acquisition, all the Jeeps and name-brand watches, all the price tags people wore. All those years, I'd denounced the notion of attaching resale value to yourself. But sitting on that train, I could now read security in what I'd only ever seen as bland, vapid inexperienced `commuters.' Something in their non-worry, their unthreatened continuum, indicated that they'd be the same in ten years. Probably right here on the 4:15 to Manhattan in updated trench coats. For the first time, that seemed good, not scary. As for me, there was no way I could repeat this performance in ten years. I'd be in mega-trouble if I was feeling this perishable at forty-six. I couldn't believe that these safe non-explorers who took two-week vacations and had hardly been anywhere were smarter than me. Nor could I believe that the creative road leads to the park bench. Nor could I find the middle ground between commitment to art (even to the point of desperation) and the simple cure-all: getting and holding onto some money.

Time passed. The ache of believing my father didn't love me slowly subsided.

I punished him by not writing him letters, but later on I thanked the man with the granite heart for the terrifying realization he donated to my cause in that fragile moment. In the material world, we're alone. I realized it later than most '60's grads, but maybe earlier than some homeless people.

I retain my faith, though, that I found on the open road and on the open seas. And I'd do it again. All of it. I'd run and hide from the corporate blob oozing from cities and malls coast to coast, I'd sample the world again and again rather than miss the Costa Rican rain forest, a Roman restaurant at 2 a.m., the Nile at sunset, the Straits of Magellan, the sound of goat bells in the Greek hills. What I got out there — seeing the world and playing my options to the last second — is the secure knowledge that I stretched my precious, adventurous, romantic youth (and vulnerability) to the max. And lived. I didn't cower, back down, or procrastinate.

Sitting on that train was the first time in my life I'd ever wished for less experience rather than more. I'd always wanted to see the world — live it, be in it, travel on my own terms, be part of the geography, feel the whole world as my home. I wanted that…I got it…to be that woman. There had never been a choice for me before.

But, ultimately, for balance, one has to have something more. Because experience, however valuable, is intangible. The bigger quest now was to find an in-between. So in that moment on the train, I guess I finally found the middle ground between `mundane life' and adventure. In that moment, I surrendered my youth.

Preparing to get off the train, I was managing my load as elegantly as possible. "I like your bag," said a young woman beside me.

I looked into her bright, open face, the one I had set out into the world with. "It looks like it's been on a lot of trips," she smiled, her eyes waiting as if I might impart a tale.

She was me. And I was the rugged world traveler, the strong one with stories whose home was the road. The wayfarer whose leather bag said it all.

I thought back to the bag's first trip thirteen years earlier, when I'd taken the Orient Express from Paris to Greece. Yet I knew it wasn't the leather bag she wanted to hear about, it was the places, the adventure, the courage to take off.

I'd become that traveler I'd wished to be. But how do you sum up a hundred journeys? Especially, when you feel you're on your last…. And you're stepping off a train into New York's Penn Station at rush hour. "There were originally two bags," I told her. "The other one wore out last summer. I cried and cried. It was my best friend."

❋ ❋ ❋

UNSCRIPTED

It seemed obvious to me that everyone wanted to be an actor. What better career was there? You got to literally be a `player,' spending your life at play. Who didn't want to play and get paid for it?

That's why acting was so competitive. Everyone wanted the parts.

So sometimes it came down to who `looked' the part. And if that part was `beautiful young woman,' then it also became a beauty contest. The glamour side of the whole business would then take precedence — droves of pretty girls strutting their stuff; and then, of course, men trying anything in their power to capitalize on the action. And that was Hollywood — no longer about talent and creativity, but seduction, manipulation, even exploitation. And endless implication.

Every woman knows her power, and in Hollywood the game is fairly blatant. Yet, despite the eternal sub-suggestion of favors, there's also an ironic underlying passion and respect for great entertainment, great movies, and great acting. And, indeed, some actresses come in like an object and go out like icon.

In NYC in the early 1970's (and still today), all the slick, shiny men wanted to cozy up to the new crop of babes—unfortunately for the girls, who were far too young to know that it all came down to skin. Stars in their eyes, they believed nice makeup, chic dresses, and vetted talent were the commodities they needed. And chicks could get crushed pretty hard by the male-controlled film industry. There was only room at the top for a rare few, no one ever quite sure how they got there, and everyone else was high on the fumes and swimming upstream.

That's why I shied away from the whole brutal scene. It was compromising, difficult, and a fuzzy kind of illusion that toyed with reality.

Anyway, how was one to get auditions with no resume? Even the Screen Actors Guild (SAG) had the barbed-wire entry requirement that you had to have performed in a SAG movie in order to join. (In other words, if you've acted in a union film, i.e. all of them, you can join the union, but you can't get a part in a union film unless you're already a member of the union.) So, I figured, even though everyone wants to be an actor, it's too hard, so most people do something else.

Under that assumption, I was waiting tables, writing, and doing black and white photography—arts where at least you didn't have to look perfect. Yet, almost by default, I kept being dated by these people, waiting on these people, and even being nudged by these people to jump on their merry-go-round. Despite this proximity, though, and my secret interest, I didn't know how to begin.

Then one day I had a bold realization: everyone did not want to be an actor. People wanted to be artists and teachers and lawyers and nurses. I met restaurant owners and cab drivers and carpenters who had zero yearning to be in movies. They'd never given acting a thought. This reorientation was jarring—suddenly my ambition wasn't universal, but distinctly mine.

But it was also liberating. A relief, actually. It meant I wasn't, in fact, competing with everybody, but really only with myself. I was the obstacle, not everyone else. Wow. For someone who likes a challenge, this had some teeth.

I took a hard look at my new odds. I was twenty-six, talented enough, nice-looking though hardly voluptuous, and probably humble enough to start at the beginning. (Now that my odds had improved.) But "Where have you studied acting?" would obviously be the first query I'd have to answer.

With a gulp, I joined a small acting ensemble in the East Village. And from there, I advanced to the renowned HB Studios in the West Village.

Famed performers had studied at HB, and every type of acting class was offered. If you had the guts and the money, you could audit a few classes, then jump in. I loved the place from day one. These people did want to be actors. And though in some ways all actors remain wanna-be's forever — always seeking their next part — some people commit to the profession. And when you see gray-haired or white-haired actors on your screen, that's them.

But acting really wasn't about playing. It was much harder than I thought. You don't merely show up and get your nose powdered, you beat the street for months and years. And when you secure a role, it's about intensive preparation. No, film and TV acting's not that playful. But it's exciting, and utterly engaging to grow a character as you rehearse.

At HB, I settled in for serious study. Students were assigned a specific scene and partner, and we'd have a week to prepare. But, since we all lived in tight Manhattan quarters, it could be tricky finding space and privacy.

At that time, I was also dabbling in fashion photography and was the manager of a prominent studio on 19th Street. The huge loft was equipped with not just the sprawling footage to accommodate fashion shoots, but a darkroom, big open kitchen, large makeup room, and a quiet, private room.

Only Pete the photographer, his assistant Joe, and I worked there, so Pete allowed Joe and me free run of the place for our own projects. Thus, my scene partner and I decided to rehearse our scene there one November evening. Joe was also there, conducting a `test' with a top NY model, but they were in the commercial space and we'd be in the private room.

'Testing' was common in fashion photography. Here, a photographer could shoot his own concepts, not for a job, and a model willing to work unpaid could end up with cool new photos for her book. (Editorial-type shots by a good photographer could show her off far better than Macy's ads.) So even well-known models always needed to update their portfolios.

After my scene partner left, and as Joe was putting his equipment away, I entered the makeup room. Part of my job was to prepare the studio for the next day's shoot — elaborate extravaganzas for which Pete was paid the big bucks.

Having completed her test with Joe, Shelley Smith (a highly recognizable, blue-eyed blonde) was in the makeup room readying to leave. "Are you an actress?" she asked, as we brushed our hair side by side. "I heard you rehearsing in the other room."

"No, but I'm studying to be. We were just rehearsing a scene for our class."

"Y'know," she said, "I'm on my way right now to an audition across the street. You should come with me."

I regarded her in the mirror, with the amazement anyone might have following that remark. This was New York City not Podunk — you don't traipse along with cover girls to their auditions.

"No, really," she persisted, eyeing my folksy attire, "I'm really not right for the part, but you are. The character's supposed to be artsy. I'm only going there to please my agent, and because it's right here, but I'm not gonna get the part. You might, though."

"Are you serious?"

"Yeah. Come with me."

"What kind of audition is it?"

"I don't know much about it, just that it's an independent film and apparently the filmmaker is doing the casting himself. That's why I think you might get in."

"It's right now?"

"Yeah."

"But how will I —"

"I'll just say you're with me." She seemed way more comfortable about this than I. "You might as well."

"Well, if you really think I'm not gonna get busted or feel totally weird for showing up there…."

"You'll be fine. I'll get you in the door, then once we're in there, just see what you can do."

"Nothing to lose," I decided.

Shelley impressed me. She didn't know me, had no personal agenda, wasn't trying to be sneaky or pull a fast one, just seemed to be putting two and two together.

So, surprising Joe, she and I left together with our combed hair and glossy lips. All we did was step out of one elevator, cross 19th Street, and step into another. And in moments, we were knocking on the door of another loft. "You don't have to say anything," Shelley whispered, "just leave it to me." The door was then opened by a secretarial-looking lady.

"Hi, I'm Shelley Smith, I have an appointment. And this is Wendy."

The lady ushered us in and told us to take seats where eight or ten empty chairs lined the walls. It was clearly the end of a long day. "Another actress is with him right now," said the lady, "but it shouldn't be long. Do both of you have appointments? I only see one name on my list."

"Well, I'm next," said Shelley, "and I guess Wendy's after me."

"Okay," said the lady, and had me add my name and phone number to her clipboard roster.

At that moment, Lisa, another princess of print, came out of the audition room, smiling broadly. She'd clearly just gotten the part. As she strode out, sprinkling stardust in her wake, the receptionist motioned Shelley to go in.

I politely waited in the now-empty room. Seriously trespassing, I wondered if a) I'd get in to see this anonymous film person, and b) what I'd say if I did.

Shelley bounced out as quickly as she'd bounced in. Seeming to know exactly who she was and what she wanted, she wasn't one to waste time. "I told him there was one more actress," she said to me. "He said you should go on in." With a wink, she left.

I went into a hallway then found an open door to a small room where a man was seated in a comfortable chair. With a nod, he indicated an empty chair across from him.

Here we go.

"Do you have a picture and resume?" he asked.

"Yes…but not with me. I only heard about this casting call on short notice."

He let that slide. "Who's your agent?"

"Um. I don't have an agent at the moment."

"You're between agents?"

"Yeah. Sort of."

He waited for more….

I just smiled.

"How did you know about this audition if you don't have an agent?"

"Shelley Smith suggested I come."

"Shelley Smith told you to come…." He waited for more.

"She said she thought I might be right for the part."

"Shelley Smith told you to come?" he repeated, scrutinizing me. "So you came here without an appointment?"

"Uh-huh." The hot water I was in was getting hotter.

"Are you even an actress?" he looked at me sideways. "How'd you get in the door?" There was a pause as he continued staring at me. "Do you know who I am? Do you know what this audition is for?"

"Okay…" I took a big breath, "here's the thing: I have no idea who you are, and I don't know anything about this film you're casting today. I don't have an agent, and I've never done any film acting. But I am studying at HB right now, and I've done theater."

"That's unbelievable. You just walked right in here? I can't believe you got this far." He studied me from head to toe. "Takes guts to just walk into an audition for a Hollywood movie without an appointment. I can't believe you."

We stared at each other, me smiling benignly as I prepared for my ouster. (At least I was the last contestant of the day, so the usual intimidating line-up wasn't swarming outside the door.)

"Yeah, I just met Shelley an hour ago. She was modeling at the photography studio where I work. She heard me rehearsing for my acting class and suggested I come with her to this audition. I'm really sorry. I apologize for not knowing about you. But that's kind of how it happened. If you want to kick me out, I understand. Or if you'd like to tell me about your film, I'm interested."

The guy then told me, with pride, that the previous year he'd won an Oscar for Best Original Song of a film he also produced and directed. Before that, he'd been successfully writing commercial jingles for a number of years. But with this recent notoriety, he was now making another film in which he'd also be starring. He seemed shocked I didn't know his name, though at least I was familiar with the hit song.

Everything about this meeting was unorthodox—his angle as well as mine. But he didn't toss me out, and even commended me on my audacity—a strong suit of his, too, apparently.

As I left, moments later, having not been asked to read any lines, I didn't regret being a gate-crasher. Sure, I got busted, but sometimes you have to walk through closed doors.

I was never to see Shelley Smith again (in person, that is—she remained all over the magazine pages), and never knew what moved her to escort me to that audition. Random acts? But, a few days later, just as I was leaving the photography studio, I grabbed a late incoming phone call. A male voice asked for me.

"This is she."

"I'm calling from the film office on 19th Street where we held the auditions. We need you to be back here at the loft at 10 a.m. on Thursday. Dress for a Christmas party."

"Oh!" I was stunned. "Is this a call-back?"

"It's not a call-back, honey, you're in the movie."

"I am?"

"Yes. 10 o'clock Thursday. Dress for a Christmas party." Click.

As it happened, that top model, Lisa, did indeed land the leading role, but I got a speaking part, too, and was in three scenes.

The guy I met on audition day turned out to be a megalomaniac, planning to catapult to fame by casting himself as the leading man. Not uber-concerned about the script (I don't believe there actually was one), he literally made up the dialogue as the filming progressed.

And as the production finished the New York shooting and made arrangements for some LA scenes, I remarked to him off-handedly, "My character wants to go to Los Angeles." Plot-wise, she was hardly needed there, but with no script, there was no determinant as to what my character did or didn't want.

Next thing I knew, I had a round-trip ticket to California with the other actors and crew. I'd only be in one scene out there, but I was elated. Because…now I'd have a film credit! Now I could join the Screen Actors Guild! Now I could keep on acting!

I did my LA scene, bade good-bye to everyone on the production, cashed in my return ticket to NY, and LA was my new home.

STEPPING OUT

Every woman pays occasional visits to the pit of self-loathing, self-pity, and fear—an emotional state where one's body, age, finances, lover, psyche, habits, and immediate future are all…unbearable!

Two Saturdays ago, I'd already cried, bathed, phoned Philly and London, tried cures from latte to wheat grass and back, and replayed my answering machine four days' worth in case I'd somehow missed that call.

Creativity dismantles this mood's wretchedness better than escapes do—if you can stand to be with yourself, but I couldn't. "Afternoon matinee, funny movie," I finally decided, willing to gamble a fifth of my life's savings for a possible chuckle.

Lacking even the pluck to dress for the public or put on mascara, I was left in loyal Levis and a pink cotton turtleneck that, like an obedient six-year-old, I tucked in. To add sneakers, then schlep down the Promenade like Ms. Everyperson, Western Hemisphere, was to only underscore my non-entity status. So—partly as punishment, partly to feel different, and partly because they were fabulous—I slipped on my new black heels. Then hid under big dark glasses.

The props didn't fool me, or diffuse my hand grenade head. In fact, negotiating the three blocks to the Promenade from where I parked the car, I could hardly walk. So wobbly and debilitated compared to my customary agility, so trapped in slow-mo, I had to pretend I was a Jackie O. or Garbo trying to divert attention—the sultry stroll saying, "Look at me," the glasses and barbed wire aura forbidding contact.

Well, needless to say, no one gave a damn. But in these me-moods, we're the center of the cosmos. And if no one stopped me for my autograph, maybe at least they said, "Cool shoes," to their step-mother.

The movie wasn't funny. And bad movies don't dispel bad moods. Would I feel lousy forever? Saturday night rolling in like a fog and I was still the drain of the known universe, its faucets full-on. Would I break my ankle getting back to the car? I sashayed out of the theatre, Uma Thurman all the way—a pair of shoulders and a pair of hipbones strung together with dissatisfaction and unpublished memoirs. But I walked as if I always walk like this, I always wear high heels, I'm a girl's girl, HUGE baby blues under these shades, darlin'. Only thing missing was Bogie.

Intense, poetic suffering—things like writing for its own sake or doing anything for a mood besides going to the gym or going shopping—are not 1990's pastimes. If you're not burning calories or credit, you're off track. Still, I claim my gender right to be bent out of shape periodically, and to do what I next did that useless eve: slid through the automatic doors at the 24-hour supermarket and slinked over to the cake stand. That store is the only one on the West Coast offering (occasionally) that particular chocolate cake with marshmallow icing, baked back on Long Island, that no one in their right mind would buy.

I wasn't in my right mind, and they had one. I snagged it.

Circling back for a pint of milk as an afterthought, I had to sneak up aisle six to the check-out since I was high-profile by now in aisle one where triathlon winners were buying Swiss chard. (Remember, I'm Focal Core of Planet Earth.)

No money for magazines, though what a women's magazine night this would make, under the covers, flavored with chocolate. Well…no time constraints on me, I hid the offender under the Sunday Times in my shopping basket and lost myself in a fifty-minute flip-through by the mag stand. I finally drowned my neurosis in a wash of photo editorials, self-help trends, horoscopes, features purporting to understand men, and the allure of slick presentation and gloss.

There is a time to be vicarious, an escape earned by just being a woman for another season.

It was great, the world dropped away. And after eating half this cake tonight, I would definitely start a new life tomorrow. Probably sell a screenplay, cycle a centennial, and save a few whales.

Taking a deep, fulfilled breath, I sauntered to check-out. Only two lanes open, and long lines. A drag for walking, my fantastic footwear proved sublime in the station, so with relative ease, I grabbed another monthly and dug back in for the duration.

Ten minutes later, I glanced up—had the cashier gone on a break? A man in the equally sluggish line next door rolled his eyes in solidarity. "Is it always this slow here?" he asked.

"Yes," I smiled.

"Oh," he shrugged. "I don't usually come here. This isn't my neighborhood; I'm just here to stock up on these," he displayed three Mexican style candles in tall glass jars. "They're only ninety-nine cents, cheaper than anywhere. These things are great, they burn forever."

It was a fine price, I agreed, and shared a noteworthy candle resource of my own. Consumer chit-chat at checkout. Then both lines started moving.

Trying to buy the cake without letting anyone see it was problematic. Passing it off as a birthday cake for someone else was implausible with that telltale pint of milk—cake for ten, milk for one? I put the glasses back on. And took a bag (paper, of course) just this once.

I regarded the candle-burner at the next cash register. His back to me, he, too, was paying. "Handsome," I thought. "Friendly." I scrutinized the oversized sweats for hints of form. Tall and slim was all I could suss.

Should I stall here at the bagging depot so we could walk out together?

"Nope!" my personal cupid all but shouted. I snatched my unfortunate parcel and headed for the door. "Do not make advances to men," scolded Cupid. "It has never worked for you. Don't do it!"

I wasn't exactly sprinting out the door, though, in those ruby slippers. And, real man that he was, he caught up with me by the door.

"Beautiful evening," I commented as we stepped into the final flames of sunset.

"The rain's really cleared the air," said he. "I couldn't believe it was raining last night. I went outside in it at four in the morning."

I told him I'd woken, too, and had checked to see if it was really raining. "Well, I better get going," I said then.

"Would you like to go have a glass of wine somewhere?" he asked, to my astonishment. Was he near-sighted and missing his specs?

"Uh, no, I better go home. I'm really tired…." I was committed to that cake. And the milk. And the coma that would follow.

"We could go just for a short while," he persisted. I took another look at his face. This man was downright adorable. Was he after my jewelry? No, I knew he was smitten by… the shoes.

"You're gonna go home and mope about not having enough romance, instead of going out with a dashing stranger??" stuttered Cupid, incredulously.

"Well, maybe we could go out just for a short while," I conceded. "It's such a beautiful night." We agreed to meet at a restaurant on the pier in half an hour, then parted.

I trod carefully back to the car; I'd been wearing those things three hours now. On the windshield was a note. From another guy, one I'd passed in both aisle one and aisle six. "A smile in the aisle," it read, on a torn off Rand McNally page. "Wanted to talk to you while you were reading magazines…. Meet me here tomorrow night at seven?"

The note was written to my shoes, I knew it. But I also knew they couldn't possibly get back here at seven tomorrow, or to the pier tonight, without a certain inhabitant who was feeling a wee bit better now.

JUNGLE FANTASY

On the Expedition, it was every man for himself, even women.

So he and I looked at each other for twenty-four days—through leaves, next to streams, across the night fire. We were both raw, climbing mountains in the mud and rain, wearing ourselves to the soul. He'd been raw from the start and never changed; I'd grown up and back down about five times, more man than woman out there, needing him but knowing he had nothing to spare. We often slept side by side, toes touching, and the last night he held me.

A jungle boy of twenty-two in Costa Rica, he used his machete as easily as a pair of hands, getting more done in a day than I could stand to watch. Obstacles, excuses, weren't known to him. Rain and cold, unnoticed. His muscles weren't separate from his bones. His eyes made the rest of the world disappear.

He'd told me he had thirty-eight acres of land and six cows. The land was an hour's walk from the sea. There was a good river that ran through, and there was good wood, he'd said. And he needed two thousand dollars to build a big house. I'd seen the house in his eyes as he spoke. He had told me these things during the Expedition, yet now I could no longer imagine any of it or even that guarded face that gave away no secrets.

He kept himself for God. For safety and sanity in the jungle, one must. And when the Expedition was over, he kissed my cheek, got on a bus, and we went separate ways.

June 15, 1985, San Jose, Costa Rica

. . . .

If I wanted to see Ernesto again, I'd have to go back to Costa Rica. And each of his letters, in all sincerity, enticed me to do so.

But it couldn't be a blind jump into the Central American void (or into the Central American combat zone, where three wars were raging). It had to be more resolute. It didn't seem so outlandish to ditch the Land of the Free and the Home of the Brave—I'd left under Nixon, and now under Reagan, I remembered why. But even my father, in his trusty scrawl, projected apprehension, "I must admit it stretches my imagination to picture you tilling the fields and milking the cows in Costa Rica as the lifestyle of your choice." What he could picture, though, read to me like house arrest, "I believe you'd be much better off sitting at your typewriter in LA."

Ernesto's world still held out a hand, but he was just a man. As my calendar seemed paralyzed at November, the jungle vividness began to feel imaginary. Was I envisioning more than there was?

Then, quite suddenly, I learned of an international peace march from Panama City to Mexico City, through all the wars. As a journalist, I arranged to cover it for The LA Weekly. This would give me seven weeks in Central America as the march crawled its way north. And if I hooked up with the marchers in Nicaragua, I could grab a few days beforehand in Costa Rica.

But the march was already underway. Only if I left right away could I fly overnight from LA to Costa Rica, take the six-hour bus ride to the east coast, then spend three or four days in Ernesto's tiny village.

The mail was slow and Ernesto had no phone. The central telephone office in Punta del Sol could give him a message that I'd call back later, and he could show up and wait for my call, but with my rudimentary Spanish, what would I say?

But I had to get a message through. I phoned twice, and even got one operator willing to fetch Ernesto's "granny" for me, since she was certain to be home. But waiting for an elder to hobble across town seemed extreme, so I gave up.

I couldn't simply appear down there, though. With only two days left before departure, I had to phone one last time. And now the operator promised Ernesto. Leaving me alone with the exorbitant rates, he sprinted off down the road.

Suddenly Ernesto's voice came through. And, hearing it, I was again on the Expedition and all my recently acquired Spanish evaporated as his voice took me back to our unspoken guessing game of the jungle.

"Ernesto…I'm coming to Punta del Sol."

"*Perfecto*," he said. "When?"

"Monday."

"*Perfecto*."

"At three or four o'clock," I went on. "I'll be on the bus from Las Palmas. Can you ask Carmela if I can stay with her?"

"Yes. And I'm sure she will say yes, or you can stay at my house."

One forgets the coarseness of all-night plane trips followed by third world bus rides, your baggage in the aisle as a seat, windows closed, tropical heat a-broil. And since I'd be in the war zones for the next seven weeks and unable to purchase supplies, I had serious equipment, from cameras, lenses, film, word processor, extra pens and paper, batteries and rechargers, to personal effects and rain gear. But, of course, when we rolled into Las Palmas on Costa Rica's east coast, an hour and a half late, the last bus to Punta del Sol had departed.

Las Palmas is a grubby, tired town. Now the sun was just setting, but not the heat. My red dress was damp and crumpled as I lumbered down the steps of the bus. A native population filled the streets, and I felt odd and out of it. There was nothing friendly or compelling about the filth or swarms of Christmas shoppers.

There was enough daylight left to get to the main road and hitch an hour south to Punta del Sol. Divulging this plan to the bus driver, though, as I disembarked, he gestured a knife slashing a throat, and recommended a hotel room and a morning bus at 5.

On the sidewalk, unresigned, I got wind of another bus going beyond Punta del Sol. Maybe it could drop me at the junction and I could somehow shuffle down that half kilometer of dirt road into town.

A string of strangers misdirected me to that bus stop and I hauled my freight over. With American goods for Carmela and Ernesto, a sleeping bag for the follow-up Nicaragua adventure, and all the rest, I was mule-like, plus sweaty, exhausted, and disgusted. Every five minutes here, where everyone was waiting for buses, zapped my impetus further. Was Punta del Sol messy like this? Was Ernesto someone special and different? I no longer trusted my memory.

Now it was 5 o'clock. Probably Ernesto was watching the other bus unload in his town square. But here in Las Palmas, we all just sighed, perspired, and watched for the bus. An hour passed. I sipped thick, sweetened orange juice, listened to Christmas carols blaring from the corner candy store, and avoided the idle eyes of a hundred faces. Unable to stand any longer, I finally swiped a chair from under a fat suitcase in the ticket office, and took out my notebook. Forty-five more minutes trudged by as significantly more passengers waited than there were seats on any bus.

Two buses finally rumbled in, and near-hysteria swept the crowd. Thundering toward the first one, they all shoved each other up its straining steps. I stood back and watched. When half the swarm was aboard, with the other half still writhing on the sidewalk like a wounded caterpillar, an official announced that the buses were marked wrong, everyone had to change. This twisted maneuver was somehow executed, mothers and babies surviving it, some even laughing. A kind man, who'd earlier assured me that a bus was indeed coming, now reappeared, took two of my bags, and pushed his way up the steps, instructing me to follow closely. Positioning me in a front seat on top of someone, he then jumped off as the bus rolled away. The person beneath me managed to move over slightly so we could share the seat. And after a chat (many of these people, of Caribbean origin, spoke English), he asked the driver (on my behalf) if the bus could maybe go all the way into Punta del Sol tonight. And the driver agreed!

This rig had open windows and the cool breeze brushed through and sedated the mob. My expectations now as rumpled and listless as my dress, I gathered fake composure before disembarking. Arriving on this ghost bus, there'd be no receiving line, but dusty little Punta del Sol would be welcoming enough.

Climbing over people, I bid my seat partner and the driver a good night and descended to the dark town square.

Loud reggae smoked from an open bar and unfamiliar black eyes lined the shadowy benches along its outside wall. More eyes edged the small park across the dirt road. By day I could've found Carmela's house, where merry faces were guaranteed, but with only a quarter moon, I'd have to ask directions. A few Rastafarians, calling to me invitingly, seemed okay to query and I started up the steps toward them.

"Wendy," I thought my name was called from the flecked darkness of the park. Looking across the road, I recognized no one on the benches. "Wendy," came the voice again, and a young boy waved. I crossed with my baggage to where Rico, Carmela's son, smiled in greeting. With him were two other boys of about fourteen, one markedly resembling Ernesto. The three boys cheerfully led me to Carmela's where my tried and true friend held out open arms.

My tedious journey melted away. We joined the melodic voices wafting through the evening, in recounting all that had transpired since the Expedition. Carmela, too, had left part of herself in that jungle, still dreamt about all of us, and still missed that…thrill of being so remote and strong. She looked wonderful and her sweet home was clean, accommodating, and spacious by Punta del Sol standards. Rico, as before, was funny, quick, companionable, and helpful. And I complimented Carmela on raising him so well by herself.

She shook her head. "No. Him not good. That's why I scold he all the time."

The other boys sat with us on the evening steps and the atmosphere contrasted sharply with my grown-up life back home. Carmela's small nieces and nephews from next door appeared for a curious peek, and behind them came Carmela's brother and mother. The weave of old and young lent humor and harmony to everything said, while the wind added a full spectrum of scent—flowers, food, the sea, and the luscious smell of clean air. Dimension was coming back to my cerebral existence.

Stealing glances at Gito, Ernesto's little brother, I wondered when I'd see Ernesto. Gito soon took leave, and Carmela and Rico now seemed eager, too, for Ernesto to arrive. It was a tiny town and there was a story in the air tonight.

Carmela's chained-up dog barked by the side of the house. "Ernesto come," said Rico. As Carmela leaned forward to look around the side, I advanced around the corner for a secluded second with Ernesto. He was leaning a bicycle against the house and patting the dog when he caught sight of me. He moved toward me, held me, and kissed my cheek. It was hurried; I turned back self-consciously to Carmela and Rico, both fully attentive.

A yellow-orange light glowed over the dark smiling faces of everyone sitting on the steps. All spoke in Spanish, Ernesto and I taking turns looking at each other. Electricity snapped between us. He was beautiful, unchanged and calm, lean and conditioned in shorts, a t-shirt, and the universal black Kung Fu slippers. Innocent and masculine, he was refined like a dancer, but his muscles were from work.

We went off together to walk in the night.

The fatigue and foreign language made things different than before. In the jungle we'd been always absorbed in commanding tasks. Out here, idly strolling down the lane, his slim, lithe stature seemed smaller.

We took the dirt road to Black Beach, past Ernesto's house, that he pointed out. Asking about his family, I learned he had six younger brothers who also lived there with their mother, and an older sister who lived in the capitol. He was chuffed I'd learned more Spanish and we used it together for the first time. "It's good," he said. "It's important for us." He taught me more as we conversed, and put an arm over my shoulder as we strolled by the sea, en route to "Ricardo's," a patio restaurant near Black Beach.

Ricardo was a sunny Rasta man playing backgammon with a Caucasian woman. Taking a table, we drank beer while a sudden rain gushed heavily down on all sides. Tired, but relaxed now, I rested my head against the hand-rail behind my stool. Entirely content, Ernesto told me how he loved the quiet life here. "All my brothers are quiet, too, like me," he said, then explained how his farmland looked out over this village, and how he wanted to build a small house first so he could stay up there three days at a time. Breathing deeply and feeling finally still after all the movement, I had little to say. How had this all happened? Suddenly here I was in the Punta del Sol night, sipping beer with Ernesto.

We talked of Nicaragua. I asked if he wanted to come with me and he readily said that he could and would.

Holding hands, we strolled back after the rain stopped. His felt small, but he squeezed mine, and we stayed that way, passing people he knew here and there. I told him I wanted to see the farm, but we didn't know when we'd have daylight hours to go there together. He said he was working every day from 7 to 3 p.m. for a man who lived in town.

Everyone was sleeping when we got back to Carmela's. Ernesto hauled a bucket from the well so I could rinse the mud off my feet, then leaned beside me on the steps. "Out of everyone on the Expedition," he said in Spanish, "I always think of you. Out of everyone."

"I will tell you something, too," I said. "I couldn't have finished the Expedition if you hadn't been there. If you had turned back, I would have also." We looked at each other. These deep bonds had never been spoken, each admitting how the other's spirit had helped carry us.

The rain was lightly falling again. "Do you think it will always rain whenever we are together?" I asked him, remembering the jungle torrents. He laughed softly.

"Should I invite you inside?" I asked.

"Sure," he replied, and followed me through the door into the two rooms Carmela had given me.

The walls were thin. Carmela and Rico sleeping inches from our whispering. A bright bulb twinkled overhead in the front room, a kitchen lacking all decor. Chilled from the rain, I slipped through the curtains into the bedroom and told Ernesto I was going to put on more clothes.

He lingered idly in the kitchen. What did he want to do now? Why had he come inside? If we were ever to get closer, the time was probably now. Wearing long pants now under my dress, I walked back over to him and put both arms around his neck. Holding me, he pulled me close, and kissed me over and over. He said short sentences in Spanish that I didn't understand. When I asked what he said, he said in English, "You know."

I didn't know.

His arms felt different than I had imagined. He was smaller, and even firmer than he looked, if that was possible. He pulled me tightly to him and kissed me with a control I couldn't resist. He moved me closer with his hands, but then stopped and looked strangely at me. He seemed to be fighting something.

"What is it?" I looked into his eyes.

He said nothing.

"Tell me," I said. "Whatever it is, I'll understand."

He stayed silent a moment, and looked small. Then, with surprise in his voice, asked, "Do you want me to stay with you here?"

"If you want to," I answered.

"Maybe tomorrow," he said, moving slightly back. He kissed my cheek and said it again, "Maybe tomorrow."

Then he left.

I remained standing there, half smiling but shaking my head. Was he concerned about the proximity of Carmela and Rico? Did his Catholicism hold him back? I fell asleep perplexed.

Next morning we were visited by Ernesto's mother, Doña Emilia. She'd come specifically to meet me and said, "Ernesto speaks constantly of you, 'Wendy, Wendy, Wendy.'" Doña Emilia was excited about her son going with me to Nicaragua, thought it was wonderful. She said Ernesto was uncertain about having enough money, though. Then, inviting me to come visit their home soon, she went off to her job at Hotel Punta del Sol, the only lodging in town.

Later that morning, Rico rode in on his bicycle. "I saw Ernesto," he said to me. "I ask him if him likes you and him says yes."

But Ernesto didn't return. Not in the afternoon, not in the evening. Carmela was concerned about my feelings and wanted to know what had happened the night before. Wondering if Rico was soaking up our porch conversation from his bedroom, I told Carmela how we'd kissed but Ernesto had seemed ill at ease.

"But," Carmela began in her comic fashion, "if a man kiss you on the lips, then him should make love with you. You must tell him: `You write that you love me—well now I want you to PROVE it!' You must go find him and tell him right now. You know I don't mind whatever you do in your room. Him tell me he wanted you to stay at his house, not my house, you know. Better you go over there right now. You want me to walk over with you?"

"Okay, let's go."

Ernesto's motorcycle was parked in front of his house. Another brother, this one a virtual clone, stepped out onto the porch of their house as we called from the yard—Carmela shouting boldly, me hiding behind her. Carmela asked for Ernesto and the brother told us Ernesto was out. "Where?" asked Carmela, with unlikely authority. The brother didn't know. "Tell him Wendy was looking for him," ordered Carmela. "Wendy the Gringa." (I was laughing now at my unanticipated role in this Italian operetta or Shakespearean drama.)

Walking home, Carmela had a good guffaw at my expense. Maybe trying to cheer me up, she said Ernesto probably didn't like me because I dress like a `rat-bat,' don't comb my hair, and am an `old lady' compared to him. Doubled over, she could hardly walk. "Look at you!" she pointed at me, doubling up again. "Your clothes are baggy like pajamas. You so skinny. He like a nice young girl with something to hold."

Thanks, Carmela.

The next morning I went grocery shopping for her. Gito, Ernesto's younger brother who'd met my bus, now ignored me in the town square. Perhaps I was imagining intrigue in the air, or did everyone know something? Punta del Sol was feeling smaller by the hour. A secret around here probably had a life-span of thirty minutes. And I now understood why no one needed phones—the children spread the word faster.

Unloading the groceries, Carmela looked at me unhappily as she finished baking the morning pies that Rico would sell around town. "Wendy, I shouldn't tell you this, but maybe it's better for you to know...."

"What?"

"Ernesto, he have a girlfriend. She live right there." Carmela pointed out the window to one of the shacks across the dirt path. "I never know nothing about this, but Rico, him tell me Ernesto love this girl and Ernesto stay always there with her at night. Sorry to tell you this." She looked crushed.

"What does she look like?" I asked, after a while.

"You can see her. She standing right there. She fat and ugly."

I peered through the translucent curtain. A light-skinned mulatto girl leaned in the doorway. She was talking to a man sitting on the porch. She was shorter than I and fuller, but hardly fat or ugly. Her face then broke into a smile and I could see she was actually quite lovely. "She's beautiful," I said to Carmela.

"Yes," Carmela now agreed. "I'm sorry."

"It's okay. I'm going to talk to Ernesto right now. I'm going over where he works and clear everything up. I'm going to ask him why he didn't tell me about her."

Of course a handsome young man would have a girlfriend. It was unfortunate she had to live forty feet from where I was staying, though. And despite all the reasoning in the world, I felt a loss.

I walked quickly—taking the back trail to avoid the town, that now felt like an x-ray machine—to where Ernesto was working in someone's yard. I needed him to be truthful with me.

A young boy in the yard went to get him.

Covered with sweat from cutting and packing cane to be used as furniture in the U.S., Ernesto walked over to me. I looked straight into his eyes. "Ernesto, what's happening?"

"Nothing," he answered blankly. "I am working."

"There's something in the air, Ernesto. What is it?"

"I don't know."

"People are telling me funny things."

"What you mean?"

"I want you to tell me what's going on."

"I don't know," he repeated. "I come over later."

"When?"

"In the evening."

Returning home, it was impossible not to observe his 'girlfriend,' still leaning in the doorway.

"What happened?" Carmela asked eagerly, as I entered the kitchen. "Did you ask him about the woman?"

"No, I couldn't—he was working. I indicated that I know, and he acted innocent."

"He playing with you. He not good. He taking you for a fool."

"Well, he didn't say anything, and said he'd come over later. I'm going to the beach."

As I left the house, the girl was watching. I ran, to get away quicker, and her eyes followed me down the road to see which way I'd go. I turned toward the beach. I had to keep cool. I felt like a fish on the shore after the tide went out. But maybe out here I could find peace.

The waves were big, the sky enormous. Palms leaned over the white sand and lined the entire curve of the bay. Gringos and natives strolled languidly by, all feeling good. The water flowed through me, then I lay on the sand and let the sun do the same. Between welcome moments of lucidity, I was truly saddened that the sweetest, purest things in life can go sour. Ernesto had seemed rare and different.

I heard voices approaching and looked up. Two women were coming along the shore, one Ernesto's girlfriend. As our eyes met, her confidence was irritating. I observed her closely as she passed. She was young and lush, rounded and warm. Her face was open and sweet, and she seemed to have merriment and mischief. No great beauty, no great mind, she'd soon be a mama. In the meantime, she was enjoying life. At thirty-five, I didn't even know what I looked like anymore. Inside I felt like I was halfway between Huck Finn and Georgia O'Keeffe—

outside I felt like the same two. If this little pineapple was Ernesto's pick of the crop, I was out of my league.

The two women joined another sunbather just thirty feet from me. I gathered my things and walked home. At least she wouldn't be staring from her porch now.

A while later, as I lay quietly on my bed, Rico entered the room. He was always whizzing hither and thither on his bicycle, busy with a million chores. Now, eyes flashing, he stood in the doorway. "There's something you should know," he said.

"What?"

"Well, you must promise not to tell Carmela if I tell you, because she be mad I told you. She be mad at me."

"Okay, what is it?"

"Okay. Not telling…I talk Ernesto today. I ask him if he like Wendy and him says no. Him say he likes girls his own age and Wendy has thirty-four."

I said nothing.

Rico went on, "You see that girl over there on the porch?" He pointed out the window, and I nodded without looking. "That's he girlfriend. She his age and he love her. He over there last night; I see him. Today he tell me that girl say if he see you one more time, she never go with him again. That's why he no come last night. He love her. She a whore, but he love her."

"When did he tell you all this?"

"Today."

"What time?"

"In the morning. I go round selling meat pies where he working and I asks him why he no come here last night, cause you was waiting. And he tell me everything. I sorry. I think he making a fool out of you, cause he in love with this girl. He no good, Ernesto."

Rico left me with this. Out my window, the woman sat on her porch again, surrounded now by children and neighbors.

I imagined what Ernesto was going through with both of us waiting for him and aware of each other. I then joined Carmela, who was separating corn kernels for tomorrow's baking. She showed me how to do it and we sifted slowly through the white chips. She was feeling sorry for me. "You know," she said, "I never see Ernesto at that girl's house — he must go at night. But I tell you, those people NEVER sits outside all day like them doing now. That house always quiet. Something funny over there."

"It's okay, Carmela. I'll be okay. It was pretty crazy to have feelings for a man so much younger than me."

"No," said Carmela. "Two people any age can have love. No. Ernesto, he do you wrong. He write you lies. You must ask him why he lie."

After we finished sifting, I didn't want to listen anymore to the voices across the road. I had only a few days in this unspoiled place before rejoining the rat-race. So I walked a long way along the seashore until the entire vista was clear of people. "Now can I cry?" I asked the Powers That Be. And my stupid little mirage spilled down my cheeks. All I could think was that everyone toeing the line in the cities was right. All those who wisely stay away from absurd love affairs that lead to Costa Rican jungles are right. They know that taking chances on exotic romance promises nothing real, is too big a gamble.

To Ernesto, I'd been like a foreign pen-pal when you're nine — I was never meant to materialize in Punta del Sol. Twice he'd even said, "I never thought you'd come back here." But why write love letters to someone you think you'll never see again? Twenty-three-year-olds can do that, I concluded.

It was hard to stop trusting something that had seemed so pure, but it seemed I had to let this go. Somewhere during my two thousand years on Planet Earth, at least I'd learned to be a happy person. And fortunately, I had the ability to get over things quickly. But I couldn't get over this while it was still happening.

Passing the hotel, I encountered Doña Emilia, who seemed jolly to see me, mothers being always the last to know. She told me Ernesto had told her he was taking me to his farm tomorrow morning. Her announcement deserved more enthusiasm than I could muster. Why was Doña Emilia so nice to me? As kind as she was, I was afraid this was our last meeting.

Continuing down the main street, Ernesto's six brothers seemed to pop continually into my view-plane. Everywhere there were Ernestos — little ones, big ones. Even people from other families started to look like at least cousins. I projected the false pride of a bad actor.

That night the heat was on. Ernesto's girlfriend's porch was alive with activity — people on the porch and in and out of the house. To create a balance, Carmela turned on loud reggae in our place. Was the whole street waiting for Ernesto? Now that it was dark, he could go unnoticed where he wished. Sitting on our back porch, I suddenly saw him walking along a perpendicular street and looking shifty indeed. I went inside to discreetly watch the house across the street from behind the curtain, to see if he'd enter from the side. After five minutes, a child ran out the front door and jumped off the side of the porch. Moments later, the child returned with Ernesto, who went quickly into the house.

Retiring completely, I tuned out on my dark bed. Why had he misled me?

Rico came in. "This not good," he said. "You must do something."

"Like what?"

"I don't know, but him making you a fool."

"I can't be made a fool, Rico, because I haven't done anything."

"What you mean?"

"I've been honest. I'm just myself. You can't make a fool of someone else, Rico, you can only make a fool of yourself."

"Why him do that then?" he asked.

"He's young, and he just wants to have a nice girlfriend. He thought he could play with me because I was far away. Now he feels foolish."

"Yes," Rico nodded. "And that girl a whore — she have lots of men."

A sound out the window broke Rico's concentration. He looked out then looked back to me, saying nothing. A moment later, Ernesto walked in. He was wearing white jeans and a light-colored t-shirt just like the figure who'd slipped into the house across the street. He crossed into the inner room where I was lying on the bed. Rico nodded to him, then quickly parted. Ernesto came and crouched at the bedside.

Feeling duped by everyone, especially him, I was still glad he'd come. He wore the untarnished innocence he always had and regarded me curiously, wondering why I was lying there in the dark.

"Ernesto," I said quietly, "what is going on?"

"I don't know."

"Everybody's talking to me about your girlfriend. Why didn't you tell me?"

"My girlfriend?"

"Yes, the girl across the street."

"She's not my girlfriend."

"She's not?"

"She's a friend."

"Everyone says she's your girlfriend."

"Who?"

"Rico."

Ernesto shook his head slowly with his eyes closed, as though this sort of thing had happened before. "What did Rico tell you?"

"He said this woman is your girlfriend and that you told him you want to stay with her, and be with a young woman."

Ernesto was still shaking his head, sadly now. "The people here is…evil. They make up crazy things. All the people here is like that. They try to hurt people. It's very bad. They make lies."

"For fun?"

"Yes, for themselves. It's very evil."

"But I saw you go in that house."

"When?"

"About an hour ago."

"That must've been my brother. He look just like me — same size. He knows her."

I studied his sincere face. "I don't believe you, Ernesto. I don't believe anybody here."

"It's true."

"What's true?"

"She's not my girlfriend. I don't have a girlfriend."

I shook my head in bewilderment. He seemed so authentic, yet I felt any moment he'd go back across the street. "I'm so confused," I lay back staring at the ceiling.

We were silent.

"Ernesto?"

"Yes?"

"Why did you write those things to me?"

"Because it's the truth," he said, looking straight into my eyes, without a trace of dishonesty.

"Really?"

"Yes," he said, as though there was nothing more to it.

Again we were quiet for a while.

"Are we going to the farm?" I asked then.

"Yes. Tomorrow morning, at 9 o'clock. Is it okay if I bring my friend Juan with us?"

"It's okay."

He was sitting on the side of the bed now. Carmela and Rico, preparing dinner outside, were leaving us alone. "Ernesto, what did you say to me the other night when we were standing there?" I asked, referring to when we'd been kissing. "Do you remember?"

"I remember," he said, smiling. "I said, `You are kind. You are nice.'"

Then I asked him about Nicaragua. He said he still wanted to come. So we talked seriously about money and it became clear we didn't have enough for us both to make the trip and both get home afterwards. But he seemed open to possibility and anxious for adventure and discovery.

Eventually, Carmela knocked and brought in a heaping plate of food for me. And the three of us sat at the kitchen table for another hour and a half reminiscing about the Expedition. We knew each other so well from our ordeal, and it was heartwarming to revisit those wild jungle days and nights, all those characters, and all that rain. An experience that penetrated the bone marrow, it could never to be fully described to those not present.

Ernesto went home around 10 p.m., saying he'd meet me at 9 in the morning.

Feeling somewhat better, I remained a bit frayed by the day's events.

Carmela was worse than a rooster, starting her day in the middle of the night. So by 9, I'd been up for hours. By ten past 9, though, Ernesto hadn't come.

Earlier, I'd spoken to Rico, and asked him why he told lies. He said he didn't tell lies. Now he was watching me, knowing Ernesto and I had been scheduled to leave at 9. I sat quietly reading as that ill feeling crept back in. By 9:30, I was thinking about a distant beach I could walk to and from there explore the next bay. It would take some mileage to walk off this twisted story. Still I sat reading and Rico left.

At 9:45, I turned to see someone hopping off a bicycle. It was Johnny, the brother of Ernesto who supposedly knew the girl across the street. "Ernesto waiting for you," he said.

"Where?" I asked, realizing only now that we hadn't set a meeting place. "At his house?"

"Yes," said Johnny. "You're supposed to come there. Him waiting."

"I was waiting for him here," I smiled.

"You wait here. Him wait there. Come on," Johnny laughed.

Ernesto was innocent again. On my arrival, he rose from where he'd been sitting against the porch wall, waiting with Juan, our chaperone. Ernesto greeted me and I explained the confusion—unfortunate since we'd wanted to beat the midday heat. He was dressed now in rough clothing for the hike, including the short black rubber boots all the men wore in the jungle, and carried his machete as he had on the Expedition. This was the man I remembered.

Moments behind me, another man arrived that Ernesto said he had to speak with for a few minutes And as the two conversed in the front yard, Doña Emilia appeared and invited me in to see the house.

It was completely unfinished, the front room empty. They'd soon be sanding the tiles, she told me, pointing to the grainy floor. A bedroom was attached to either side of this room—one hers, the other Ernesto's, from which loud Costa Rican music billowed. All was open and sunny. We followed a hallway to the back yard, where an outside eating area was book-ended by the two bedrooms of Johnny and Oscar. In the yard all was still—no neighboring houses, just trees, greenery, and a tiny unit with a toilet. The air of complete tranquility was reflected in each face as well. Four of Ernesto's brothers were home, each as striking as the next. Sweetness, grace, long brown legs, strong arms, and soft black eyes everywhere.

Doña Emilia told me that when I came to stay here next time all would be much nicer. Then Roberto, the youngest, brought me a tall glass of water, as Johnny presented the cherished family photo album, pointing out, page by page, shots of Ernesto growing up. Mildly embarrassed, I wondered how this clan viewed my relationship to Ernesto. If anybody knew the truth, it had to be them, yet they all treated me like I belonged there.

Doña Emilia now led me back to the front porch where we embarked on a long conversation about life, nature, and God, as Ernesto continued chatting with the man in the yard. Though Doña Emilia spoke in Spanish, I understood every word and she understood me. Our talks were always like journeys we both hated to end.

Finally at 11:00, Ernesto concluded his business and we set off with Juan.

We took the dirt road to the main road that went to Las Palmas, then crossed over it onto a muddy path. Ernesto in the lead, we climbed steadily for nearly an hour. The jungle wasn't thick like the untouched rainforest we'd traveled through in Karakima, but the plants were the same and the climb felt divinely familiar.

Once we were well inside the jungle, we slowed down and Ernesto began pointing things out to me. Whatever his weaknesses, they were gone now. He had total fluidity of movement and the keenest observation. He picked up a hundred details that my recent city time now obscured from me, acknowledging exotic birds and plants as we walked. He followed a vine into the earth and pulled up twenty yams. He dug under another tree, pulled up its root and held fresh ginger to my nose. He jumped and grabbed a low-hanging orange, peeled it perfectly with his machete, and handed it to me. Glancing down, he stooped quickly to scoop something up. "Open your hands," he said and dropped into them a teeny frog with jade and black markings on its back. There were cacao plants and coffee. Ernesto broke open the fruits of each for me to taste. At one point, he quickly grabbed me and gestured to a distant tree. Pawing up its side was a sleek, black, mink-like mammal, who darted away at the sight of us. Ernesto showed us which trees were light-weight for making boats and which were heavier for building houses.

Climbing higher, he let us know when we were crossing land that belonged to someone, usually one of his brothers. And higher still, by noon we'd reached the top where Ernesto's land began. So pleased to be there, his pride and love for every inch of it set him aglow. We continued along a ridge to where he said the view was best, then gazed out across the jungle we'd come up through, rolling all the way down below to where the village met the sea. `The Point,' a promontory of beach, was clearly outlined, and white-caps striped the blue water where the reef was. The only sounds were the pure ones of the jungle. "*Muy tranquilo*," said Ernesto, looking out across it all to the sea. "No one can bother you here."

"You couldn't ask for more," I said. "What more is there?"

"Nothing," said Ernesto.

We then cut back along the ridge to another overlook where the long branch of a tree served as a bench in the shade. As we snacked on oranges, Ernesto talked of his plans and all the work he wanted to do. He'd put the small house right here where we were sitting, he said.

We then continued up to another rise facing the other direction. This hill was almost grassy and overlooked a valley of dense foliage with mammoth trees and tall palms. Below, said Ernesto, was a small river, and up the other side was where the big house would be. He spread his arms wide. All this land was his.

And off in the distance, to the west, rose layers of mountains. "Karakima?" I looked nostalgically toward the untouched, cloud-draped peaks.

"Yes," said Ernesto, "the mountains we crossed."

Lying on the hillside beneath a towering tree, an overdue serenity claimed me. The sounds were all pure — a bird calling, a branch dropping from the jungle ceiling, the wind rustling through, our voices, Ernesto's machete clearing the growth around us. We were so safe from humankind. And Ernesto wanted his whole life this way.

He spoke often of money, or `plata,' as it was called. He needed two thousand dollars to have the wood cut for the house. That's why he was working so hard in town. Seeing this land and hearing his hopes for it, I knew he wouldn't be spending money on a trip to Nicaragua.

In time we started back down. Moving quickly, we only stopped once for more oranges. Forty-five minutes and we were back in Punta del Sol.

Covered with sweat, I was heading directly for the waves. As we reached the fork where we'd separate, Ernesto asked if I wanted to meet his father that evening at 7 o'clock.

"Okay," I agreed.

"Do you know where he lives?" Ernesto asked.

"Right next door to your house, right?"

"Right. Seven o'clock."

"Okay. Thank you for showing me your farm."

"It was nothing."

Today the house across the street was silent. Everything was like it had been before, Carmela said, quiet.

At 7, I strolled over to Ernesto's. His father, Arnoldo, was there expecting me, and spoke fluent English. Ernesto, he told me, had gone out. And in his next breath, he said he'd heard a lot about me and had read all my letters.

"You read all my letters to Ernesto??" My astonishment was as great as my embarrassment.

"Yes," Arnoldo smiled at my incredulous stare. "And I saw all the photos you sent." The photos were of the Expedition, and I apologized for the lousy quality of the xeroxed slides. This turned the conversation to photography — thank God. Arnoldo was a photographer, too, he told me.

This man was utterly gracious. We spoke of war and peace for about two hours — his perspective unusual, his vocabulary odd but impressive. Ernesto never returned, and from time to time I lost my train of thought, wondering what I was doing here alone with the father of a man who'd publicized my intimate letters.

I told Arnoldo I was sold on his entire clan, and would love to photograph each one. I'd met them all now, including little Oscar, who had just graduated from high school but looked about seven. "He just stayed little like that," Arnoldo laughed. "Nobody knows why. It's funny," he laughed again. "He's even littler than his tiny little granny, and you should see her…." He then called into the open doorway of the house, "Mavis?" A little old lady appeared in the doorway. It seemed we'd distracted her from something she was doing inside. "See her?" Arnoldo mused at her shortness, then told her she could leave now, he'd just wanted me to see how short she was. She turned and left.

"Does the family live in two houses?" I asked.

"Yes. We're all together really, but there are a lot of us so we have two houses. Mavis lives here with the two youngest children, because they are the ones that are home the most, so they can take care of each other. I have my darkroom here, so I work late a lot and usually sleep here, too. Doña Emilia and the older boys all live next door. And they all work during the day." This seemed extremely sensible.

"So you're thinking of taking Ernesto with you to Nicaragua?" Arnoldo asked me.

"That's up to Ernesto."

"Yes. And I think he should go with you. He's over twenty-one now and should get out into the world a bit. It's a good opportunity for him to learn about things. But he seems to have misgivings about whether he can manage it." Something in his tone led me to believe I was being given a message from Ernesto. And a few moments later, as I was preparing to leave, Arnoldo said, "Maybe Ernesto will change his mind and go with you...."

The next day, the alleged girlfriend resumed her post in the doorway, seeming to watch our place. I decided to dismiss it all and spend a mellow day with Carmela and her sharp mind, understanding, and good jokes. Though an odd duo, we were allies forever after our tour in the jungle.

Late that night, I was on the porch when a man in a hat emerged from the house across the street. He seemed to see me but kept walking. He was about Ernesto's size, but I didn't think it was he. Then he turned back, saw me still on the porch, and stopped and waved. Taking off the hat as if to make his identity clearer, he moved closer. I walked across the yard to the fence. "*Hola*," he said.

"Oh, Juan, it's you," I recognized Ernesto's friend from our hike to the farm. "What's up?"

"Not much," he answered casually.

I strolled along beside him down the silent trail. "Who lives in that house?" I asked.

"Una amiga," he answered. ("A female friend.") Stopping at the corner, where I'd turn back, we were standing close enough for the strong smell of beer to waft from Juan to me. I couldn't ask him any more questions, but Carmela had mentioned seeing lots of different men frequenting that house.

The following morning I walked miles along the shimmering coast. The jungle grew right down to the sand line and in places palms actually grew right in the water. But where vegetation interrupted the shoreline, a trail could be followed just inside the edge of the jungle. Here, birds and monkeys twittered and hollered. Footprints and horse tracks showed that others had passed, but I was blissfully alone. Continuing on, I rounded The Point to find another stretch of pristine beach, with not a soul as far as the eye could see. So I ran and danced across the sand, sang, leapt over driftwood logs, skinny-dipped and lay in the sun, Not exactly the setting for feeling forsaken.

Before leaving in the morning, I needed a moment alone with Ernesto. He should tell me himself what he felt. So that afternoon, I walked over to his house. As I arrived, Ernesto was just pulling up on his bike. A contagious stiffness crept from his body over to mine, as I greeted him and he returned half my smile.

"I'd like to talk with you a little," I said. "Can we go for a walk or something?"

He indicated that right here in front of the house would be alright.

I'd decided that an apology from me might extract one from him. "Ernesto, I feel bad that I've made things uncomfortable for you...."

"Oh, it's no problem," he softened. "It's no trouble for me. You have friends here—Carmela and me, and others.

And you have lots to do, lots of places to go…the beach, the mountains. Some people come here all alone and they still have a good time. There's lots to do in Punta del Sol."

"And what about Nicaragua?" I asked, wanting him to tell me himself.

"Didn't my father tell you?"

"No. Why did you want me to meet with your father anyway?"

"Because my father speaks English, so he could explain better why I can't go to Nicaragua."

"He didn't explain."

Ernesto was surprised. "Well…I'm not going because I'm afraid of the war. My friends tell me Nicaragua's dangerous, so I won't go. I don't want to die."

"Nicaragua's not the problem. El Salvador maybe. Anyway, it's your decision. I'm not afraid and I am going at 6 in the morning. Ernesto, why did you write those things to me?"

He was quiet. He looked into my face, then let out his breath and in careful Spanish said, "In Spanish, we say `I love you' to our friends. When we have strong feelings of respect, of gratitude, of closeness, we say 'I love you.' We, in Costa Rica, love very much, with deep sincerity. We love our friends. And I feel this way about you. Of the deepest, sincerest nature." His hand was over his heart, his eyes were earnest.

"I understand," I smiled at him. "It's important, Ernesto, to speak about these things. It's important always…for friendship."

"Yes," he agreed, "it's very important." He was relaxed now, having lightened his load.

Love is like business; for it to flourish, the terms must be clear. Ernesto could've saved me an exhausting trip by stating his truth in a letter. Disappointed, I didn't feel like hugging him or even shaking his hand. His strength and beauty and love of nature, not to mention our epic experience together, assured him a place in my heart, but for now he was a twenty-three-year-old boy straddling a bicycle.

From opposite ends of the spectrum, maybe we'd learned the same lesson—something about overblown fantasy and misplaced passion. Or maybe we didn't yet know what the lessons were.

As I strolled back along the dusty main road, peopled as always with Ernesto's brothers, I silently thanked him for the best broken heart I'd ever had. Punta del Sol, the beaches, the jungle, and the people here, were way worth the trouble.

Doña Emilia now rounded a corner and waved happily to me. We stood chatting in the main square, as though we'd been close for years. Speaking Spanish with her was effortless. She told me she was thoroughly disappointed that Ernesto wasn't going to be traveling with me. "He's twenty-three," she said, "and his father and I both tell him he should go out into the world. He's a man now. But he doesn't want to leave the house. This is a great opportunity for him to learn something. But he's involved with the Catholic Church. He was there last night and someone told him that if he died in Nicaragua, the spirit of Christ wouldn't go with him." She broke out laughing and I joined her. Then we both laughed harder and she slapped her knee. When we stopped, she went on, "Ernesto is a very humble person," she cradled her arms as though remembering him as a baby. "He always has been.... He's very...very...." she couldn't find a word.

"He keeps a lot inside," I volunteered.

"Yes. Everything. He's never told me very much. Never. Ernesto's like a child still. We want him to grow up but he doesn't seem to want to. He likes you very much, but he's afraid he'll die in the war."

"I care for him very much, too, and I know he likes me, but probably as a friend, not as a woman. And maybe on a long trip it would be difficult. I don't think he's really afraid to die. He wasn't afraid on the Expedition. Maybe it's also a problem of money."

"Yes, the money's a problem. He had decided to sell one of his cows, but when the man arrived to buy it, he wanted to pay later." Doña Emilia laughed again. "But I don't think it's a problem of money because Ernesto said to me many times, `Mama, if Wendy asked me to go to Los Angeles, I'd go in a minute, but not Nicaragua.'"

When I told her I was leaving in the morning, she grew sad and asked when I'd be back. I had to say I didn't know.

"When you come back," she said enthusiastically, "the house will be all finished and you will stay with us." With her hands, she illustrated a smooth and perfect home with everything just right.

"Okay," I agreed.

"Are you coming over tonight?" she asked, as I was leaving.

"I don't think so," I said, trying to make it sound open-ended.

That evening, I took a last sunset walk along the shore, then headed back to Carmela's along a small dirt road. People on their porches were enjoying the evening. Up ahead, a man walked toward me from the other direction. Coming closer, I saw it was Arnoldo. We were glad to see each other. As with Doña Emilia, I'd found him instantly likable. We shook hands in greeting. "Are you enjoying the evening?" he smiled.

Arnoldo seemed to have a bright light burning inside. With no excess energy or unnecessary movement, his face was radiantly alive. His smile was so wide and ready, his eyes so attentive, and his mind so quick, that it was nearly impossible not to giggle in his presence. He seemed to want to romp and play, his trim physique as agile as Ernesto's. Typical father of eight, he wasn't.

"Yes, I'm having a nice walk," I answered. "And I'm very happy to see you. In fact, I was just thinking about you and your beautiful family. And I wanted to tell you how nice it has been to meet you all."

He beamed a little more, "When are you going to Nicaragua?"

"Tomorrow morning."

He nodded.

"Ernesto told me today that he's not going to Nicaragua," I said then.

"Yes, that's right," said Arnoldo. "I told Ernesto it was up to him but he says he's afraid of getting killed."

"He was fearless in the jungle," I said. "I think he's afraid of me."

Arnoldo laughed.

A friend of his strolled along then, so we said goodbye. "I might see you in the morning before you go," Arnoldo said.

"The bus leaves at 6," I smiled.

"Sometimes I'm up at quarter to 6," he smiled back.

My last evening was spent with Carmela and the wicked Rico. Who would ever know whether it was he who'd lied or Ernesto? Regardless, Rico was delightful company — hungry for every detail of the world beyond Punta del Sol. Tonight the three of us discussed Rico's aspiration of working on a big ship someday. Carmela told morbid tales of innocent little sailors getting busted for the cocaine other sailors had concealed in their bunks. But, wanting to see dreams reach fruition, I reminisced about the whales, dolphins, flying fish and icebergs I'd seen at sea; about stars all the way down to the horizon; about being rocked to sleep and waking in foreign ports. Rico listened wide-eyed. The dog barked outside, announcing a visitor. Rico went to the window, and reported back that Arnoldo and Doña Emilia were here.

Dressed in their evening best, as I hadn't seen them before, they'd come to say farewell and wish me a safe journey. Carmela and I were both moved to see them.

We brought chairs onto the porch and spent a charmed hour in mixed English-Spanish conversation. Arnoldo presented me with a photograph he'd taken of a carnival in Las Palmas. Artistically, it left something to be desired, but emotionally, it filled me. In exchange, I gave them candles and peanut butter — without saying they'd originally been for Ernesto.

"Did Ernesto come by tonight?" they asked.

"No," I answered.

"He hasn't been here in three days!" Carmela fumed, rolling her eyes.

"Carmela," I put a hand on her arm.

But Arnoldo and Doña Emilia looked unhappily at each other. Then Doña Emilia got up and walked around the side of the house. Carmela and I both knew she was looking across the street to see if he was on the porch over there. She then returned, shrugged to her husband, and sat back down.

Again the parents spoke of how worthwhile it would be for Ernesto to accompany me. There seemed to be disappointment about him all the way around. "One day he'll realize what he missed..." Arnoldo said, looking into the distance, "but it will be too late."

My happily-ever-after-in-the-jungle illusion died and went to heaven. In the jungle with Ernesto, I would have done whatever had to be done. A man needs a woman up there. Genders are clearly delineated, plus in that strong environment, it's important to feel cared for. Out there before, we had shared something elemental, we'd been in sync with the natural order. But here in this town, Ernesto had his job, his church, his brothers, friends, bicycle, motorcycle, maybe even a girlfriend. Society itself seemed to separate us, pointing up our differences, ones we'd had no occasion to notice before.

Still, in the grand expanse of life and love and the jungle, and certainly on the Expedition, Ernesto had shown me purity, honesty, strength, and solidarity. Here in the `real' world, our backgrounds kicked in, almost like bad lighting on beautiful memories.

Perhaps, ultimately, these few days in Punta del Sol spared me a tougher realization later—that, just as he was a young man in a tiny Costa Rican village, I was a grown woman more reliant on my own culture than I wanted to admit. Maybe tilling the fields and milking the cows was a complete fantasy. Maybe I was better off in LA sitting at my typewriter....

But that majestic landscape, even just for its own sake, remains majestic indeed.

WORKING THE PARTY

The current backdrop was Hollywood. And my friend, Esmé, had a remarkable aptitude for sniffing out power moguls. With me as her sidekick, we were not to be impeded.

Esmé was larger than life—a voluptuous 5'10", with long thick blonde hair and a movie star face. She loved low-cut dresses, high-cut heels, and thrived on crimson, turquoise, saffron, lime, and violet. Navy blue, beige, brown, and muted greens were insults to her palette. And if you overlooked her out in the general public, there was something seriously wrong with you. In response to the question constantly posed of her, "Why aren't you an actress," she'd figured out early on, and told me, "I don't have to be a movie star; people already treat me like one wherever I go."

True dat. And, though not exactly a wallflower myself, beside Esmé I was invisible. We weren't in competition though; in Hollywood in 1978-79, there were plenty of parties, dates, jobs, and excitement to go around. A giant, frisky generation was running with the ball.

Esmé also had the knack of befriending people that I found unlikely chums. I was drawn more to sporty, beachy sorts to swim and dance with, commiserate or cavort with. But after having tea with Esmé's cohorts at her apartment (across the hall in Venice Beach), or going to brunch with them, I began to comprehend her motives. She was an ambitious film school grad, and all her connections had to do with filmmaking. I never knew where she lassoed these producers and studio executives, but then again Esmé was several rungs above me on the mover-and-shaker ladder, and one always wonders how the next tier does it. The social whirl seemed as intrinsic to her as hot pink and chartreuse, and her looks hardly shooed people away. Thus, a constant cast of characters cha-cha-ed through her life.

But for me, the friendship with Esmé — one of the great ones in my life — had little to do with all that. Though we didn't actually meet till our mid-twenties when we both lived in Manhattan, not only did we instantly click, but we were the same age, both in the film business, both from the tiny town of Amagansett, and…Esmé, at age twelve, had been my mother's best friend.

Mom had now been gone ten years, but I still recalled her telling me back in 1962, "You're not gonna believe this, but my best friend is your age!" In our waterfront village, populated back then mostly by artists and fishermen, Esmé and Mom had both taken a summer oil-painting class on an old barge. And once they became pals, Esmé had car-pooled with Mom. So it was ever heartwarming to hear Esmé affectionately remembering my mother.

Ibrahim Moussa was one of Esme's passing playmates. The tall mustachioed Egyptian loved to throw parties at his mansion up in the canyon. His English was quick and clever, and he happened to be a producer with offices at Paramount. Ibrahim knew people, and his recent ex of three years was a big star. Next thing I knew, we were not just invited to his soirées, but were special guests. Moussie, as we fondly dubbed him, soon considered the two of us intimates that no gathering was complete without.

One night we were wining and dining chez Moussie when he casually announced that `Omar' was flying in tonight and would be staying at his place. Esmé and I may have passed each other a look, "Omar?"

An hour or so later, Moussie lightly said, "Omar just called, he's at the airport." He then glanced around the room, sort of thinking out loud, "…I really should stay here — can someone else go and pick him up?"

"We'll go," I said breezily, as Esmé regarded me with surprise (we will?).

"You will?" Moussie, though equally surprised, was glad to have recruited drivers so easily.

"Whose car do we take?" asked Esmé, possibly concerned that neither of our two beaters would measure up to the assignment.

"Mine," said Moussie. "Take the Rolls."

As Esmé balked ever so slightly, I said, "Fine, let's go."

Moussie, right on my page, dug the keys out of his pocket. Esmé seemed to feel under-qualified for the gig, or maybe nervous about borrowing the Rolls. But I knew this was the type of task you must take nonchalantly before someone better suited — like a chauffeur — jumped in. Moussie tossed us the keys.

Stepping into the cool night air, Esmé half whispered, "It's Omar Sharif, y'know." Omar Sharif was a big celebrity at the time, after having received international acclaim for the title role in the movie, `Dr. Zhivago' (winner of five Oscars).

"Yeah, I figured. Not too many Omars runnin' around. Who's driving?" We approached the gleaming prize in the drive.

"I will," said Esmé, herself again, now that the mission was underway.

"Good," I said, relieved not to be the one to run it into a ditch. She was bigger anyway and could probably use the experience for future drives in other Rolls Royces.

So off we set, the two of us gliding down the dark canyon toward LAX. It would take us about half an hour, and apparently Omar would meet us at the curb. Obviously, we'd recognize the guy, and obviously he'd spot the car.

Esmé and I were having a giggle about being consigned to "go get Omar." Even though he was a bit older than us, and we weren't deliriously star-struck, it was still an agreeable chore.

"I think we should do something with him while we have him all to ourselves," I said mischievously.

"Like what?" Esmé liked the idea.

"I dunno. But it seems kinda stupid to just drive him straight back to the party, don't you think?"

"Yeah, now that you mention it. But what're we gonna do with him?"

We had to laugh.

"Well..." I couldn't think of anything particularly exotic, "...why don't we kidnap him?"

"Kidnap him?"

"Yeah."

"Like, hold him hostage?"

I was laughing pretty hard now, picturing Omar Sharif bound and gagged in the trunk of the Rolls or in Esmé's closet. "Yeah, right, and demand ransom from Moussie. No, no, I don't mean kidnap him for money, just for fun. We could take him somewhere."

"Against his will?"

"I have a feeling it won't be against his will to be kidnapped by two blondes in a Rolls."

"You're probably right," Esmé chuckled, "but we don't really know anything about the bloke."

"We will after we kidnap him. Anyway, we do know him, he's Dr. Zhivago. How weird could he be?"

"So how do we do it?"

"Don't worry about that, that's the easy part. I'll break the news to him, as long as I know you're down with it."

"I'm down," said Esmé.

Content with our agenda, we were soon entering LAX. We might not get back to the party as swiftly as Moussie expected but, again, those weren't the kinds of details people concerned themselves with in the 1970's in Hollywood.

As we eased up to the curb where arriving passengers were milling about, Omar spied us instantly and waved. Yes, indeed, the handsome Dr. Zhivago. And friendly.

"Hi Omar!" we said, "Hop in!"

"Hello," he said happily.

"Moussie sent us to pick you up," said Esmé.

"I hope you don't mind," I added, testing the waters.

Omar stepped into the back seat. "I don't mind at all. In fact, I'm very pleased."

"Good," said Esmé, easing into the traffic flow.

"Yes, good," I affirmed. "And I hope you also won't mind that we're going to kidnap you."

"You're going to what?" He thought his inexpert English was deceiving him. (Another Egyptian.)

"We're going to kidnap you," Esmé repeated. "Right now."

"Oh good!" said Omar. "That sounds delightful!"

"Well, you certainly have a positive attitude for a kidnap victim," I commended him. "Do you have experience with abduction?"

"Yeah," said Esmé, "usually our victims don't respond this well."

"You do this often?"

"No, you're the first," we admitted.

"Where are we going?" asked Omar then, even more excited about the kidnap than we.

"Well...." Esmé trailed off.

"Well...." I did the same. "We haven't selected a destination yet."

"Any suggestions?" asked Esmé.

"We could go have a drink," offered Omar, beyond compliant. He loved the turn his evening had taken and said we could do with him whatever we fancied.

We decided to drive into Hollywood and see what appeared. Esmé and I were lucky our captive was so easy going—he seemed blissed out to just cruise up and down Melrose Avenue.

Having a drink was hardly the most risque kidnap on record, but a safe and pleasant one. We went to `El Coyote,' sat in one of the red booths and sipped margueritas. Omar was all in and even picked up the tab—beyond the pale really. And then we took the Rolls back up the mountain to its stable.

Moussie seemed a bit confused by the time lapse since our departure. But he was generally mellow, especially when the three of us acted like stopping for a drink was the customary thing to do.

So it wasn't a kidnap for the tabloids or the morning news, but Esmé and I felt we pulled it off rather well.

A year or two later, I ended up living and working in London, and was lucky enough to sign with William Morris, a major talent agency with an impressive roster of actors. One night, my agent invited me to a private client dinner— not one of the gala holiday events the agency threw, but a sedate evening for just a few clients and agents. At this dinner, in a private room of a finer London restaurant, were gathered maybe a dozen of us. And only a few minutes after being seated, in walked Omar, another of their clients.

With some pride, my agent introduced me to the big star (who, needless to say, I hadn't stayed in touch with). Concealing his surprise, Omar kissed my hand.

"We've met," he smiled.

"Yes," I smiled back. "Indeed we have."

My agent seemed to expect an explanation, seeing as I was American from LA, and Omar was Egyptian and lived in London, but no explanation was offered. Kidnappers aren't known for boasting about their conquests, and kidnap victims are woefully ashamed should they experience any pleasure during their ordeal.

✳ ✳ ✳

"You have to lower your standards to have fun in life — but you will."

~ Elizabeth Dillon, my HB acting teacher

THE WRITER

In 1980, London had become home for the second time. Nearing thirty, I was both terrified of and committed to the artist's life—diligently focused on my acting career, while secretly appreciative that the frequent down-time, combined with the generous wages, afforded ample hours, sometimes even months, to work on my first book.

The way one becomes a writer, a real one, is to write from the gut and heart, and to do it often enough that, like anything well-practiced, one becomes competent. Others may judge the craft by quantity produced, quantity published, income earned, or status on bestseller lists, but real writers—like real painters, real dancers, real musicians, real singers, real woodworkers—judge craft by its emotional effect on consumers, its authenticity, its originality, its beauty, and its endurance. As with Fred Astaire's dancing, talent isn't a magical thing, but acquired through patience, practice, dogged determination, and sacrifice. You gotta want it for all you're worth.

So I was writing the second draft of "I Did Inhale—Memoir of a Hippie Chick," that would reach at least fifteen drafts and have three different titles before it was published a mere thirty-five years later. And I could oft as not be found scribbling in a local cafe or tapping the keyboard in my bedroom. The cool thing about any stage of being a writer is the ongoing gratification it provides its creator, even if only getting down a few pages. I wouldn't call it victorious or philanthropic or adventurous or orgasmic — there are grander satisfactions than expelling emotion or confusion onto a page — but for expression, for self-satisfaction, and for high-yield work investment, writing is rewarding.

It was winter in North London. I'd escaped tyrannical love by moving out of the boyfriend's flat, to now share a large, two-story place with three other people. And recently, a young woman I'd met on the Greek island of Xaxos had turned up and we'd rented her a room while she plotted her next move.

Paulette was a well-intentioned vagabond, at odds with the world of work and wages, but a gentle reminder of the clean white life we'd led in stone houses overlooking the Aegean. She had even lasted a full winter there, and was one of the few foreigners who, like me, had fallen in love with the language as well as the island and people. Her musical laugh overshadowed her financial blind spot and, like many, she'd cultivated methods for getting by on virtually nothing. Her approach was to maintain a network of fellow travelers (myself included) to stay with when she showed up in their home cities, states, or countries.

One day, Paulette mentioned that there was this young guy, Jonathan, who'd also spent time on Xaxos, who'd recently arrived in London. She said he was also a writer and that he'd apparently met me on the island. She asked if I remembered him, but I couldn't say I did.

A week or so later, she mentioned having met with him again and that, while in Greece, he'd finished writing his first book. Now he'd like to rendezvous with me since we were both writers who'd completed a book.

I really didn't view myself as `a writer' yet, more a loyal servant to a passion. Being `a writer' was decades down the pike, probably posthumously; right now it was merely about process. And I didn't feel the need for writer-connection that maybe Jonathan did. But that was probably due to my having other work in London, plus friendships, and even that pain-in-the-butt heart-throb. But I told Paulette to invite Jonathan over and we'd all have tea.

When he arrived, I knew I'd met him briefly before, but gray London winter casts a different hue than that blue-white shimmer we'd known. Jonathan was amiable enough, though. Almost twenty-one and already done with his first memoir, he smiled in recounting how his grandfather had scoffed, "How can you write your memoirs when you haven't even lived yet?" There could be some truth to this, but good writing is good writing.

Manuscript in hand, young Jonathan readily unfurled it for me. Back then, there was even more pride attached to having one's own crisp, white, literary stack of pages because, with every word hand-typed, editing took ridiculous elbow grease. (I'm not even sure we had correcting fluid or Wite-Out yet—this may have still been back in the carbon paper days.) But even then, the proof was in the pudding. "I was wondering," he began humbly, "if maybe you would read my book and tell me what you think of it...."

I've never been the professorial type and, less than eager to read the thing, sort of waited for what else he might say. Hopefully I could find a polite way to pass.

"I really don't know anyone else who I think would be appropriate to ask. I thought, since you're also writing about your own life experience and you've been writing much longer than me, that your opinion would be valuable."

I felt, and will always feel, compassion for anyone who's not only moved to write a book, but actually does it. Plus, who knew, maybe Jonathan's was a masterpiece. If nothing else, any friend of Xaxos was a friend of mine. "Okay," I agreed, "but give me a little time because I'm in the middle of some other stuff. I'll read it, though, and let you know what I think."

Jonathan was elated. And I knew all too well what it means to go public, especially regarding a first draft of a first book.

It was a tidy, well-typed chronicle at least, all I had to do was read. So, even though I'd been allotted time, I surrendered to my assignment the next day. Climbing into my wintry bed with a cup of English tea, I began Jonathan's book.

I can't recall the title, though I remember thinking it a bit soggy. However, Jonathan had mentioned that he was open to changing that and anything else I might point out. I felt a tad over-valued by him, but also knew I was as unbiased as any reader he'd find and could comment adequately on the readability, grammar, story line, and character development of a new writer's work. And it shouldn't take too long. (Maybe I could even genuinely help him, as a couple of my early readers had me.)

Page one.... "Okay..."

Page two.... "Hmm."

Page three...."Hmmm."

Page four...."Oh dear."

Page five...."I'm in trouble."

I couldn't even turn the next page. I could read no more. This book was just awful. So far, it lacked pretty much everything one needs from a book.

So I flipped ahead a few chapters.

More sophomoric outpouring of shapeless events.

I thumbed ahead toward the book's end…. Same.

There was no hope for this book. Jonathan clearly had no writing experience whatsoever. His book had no redeeming qualities. It was so unreadable I couldn't endure one more paragraph.

I closed the manuscript and placed it at one side of my long desk, then carefully took another week before phoning the fellow.

"What'd you think?" he hungrily asked over the phone.

"Well…" I paused, already knowing what I was going to say, "why don't you meet me at the Heath Cafe to pick up your book, and we'll talk then?"

He agreed, and the next day we sat down for coffee.

As anyone would be, Jonathan was ready to hang on my every word. He was also visibly hopeful, young as ever, and still a friend of Xaxos.

"Well?" he began.

I handed him his document. "Well," I said slowly, "first let me say congratulations—you finished writing a book. That in itself is a major accomplishment that most people never achieve. And you're only twenty-one."

"You didn't like it."

"I didn't say that…."

"You probably couldn't even read the whole thing. How far did you get?"

"I read the whole thing."

"You did? Well, what'd you think?"

"I'm going to tell you, but first let me finish what I was about to say."

"Okay."

"I really want to impress upon you how important it is to have completed a first draft like you did."

He nodded.

I continued, "Now…you do realize, don't you, that every book, every book, requires multiple drafts? So I don't feel bad telling you that you have to write another draft of this book. That's just a fact."

"You didn't like it."

"I did like it."

"You did??"

"Yes."

"Really?"

"Really."

"You're not just lying to me to make me feel good?"

"Nope."

Jonathan stared at me in disbelief.

"It's good," I said. "You've got the start of good book. You just need to keep working on it. But I believe you can and you will."

He was now satisfied. The book was good. He didn't even press for details.

"You'll keep working on it, right?"

"Yes," he said, "I definitely will."

Soon we said adieu, and I got back to my own sophomoric scribbling.

I didn't keep in touch with Jonathan, though I may have received a post card from him at some point. He continued on his travels. And soon even Paulette had been absorbed by France or Oregon or some other port-of-call where she had a friend.

It was a year or two later that I returned to Xaxos and all its splendor. As always, I was up to my neck in olives, tomatoes, goat herds, Aegean bliss, stony hillsides, writing, and dancing. One afternoon, as I walked through the quaint portside village where everyone gathered for food, greetings, and gossip, someone walked right up to me, stopping me in my tracks.

"There you are!" said he. "I've been looking for you!" It was Jonathan, literally blocking my path.

"Oh, hi Jonathan!"

"I'm really mad at you!"

"You are? Why?"

"Because you told me my book was good. Why did you tell me that?"

I said nothing. Obviously there was more to come from the young author. Fuming, he went on, "Why did you lie to me? The book wasn't good. It was horrible."

"What makes you say that?"

"Because after I left London, I showed it to a couple of other people, because I thought it was good. And they told me it was awful! It was NOT a good book and I don't understand why you told me it was. I even submitted it to a publisher and he told me it was unreadable!"

I was lucky Jonathan didn't have a gun.

"Are you still writing?" I asked him.

"Yes...." he looked at me accusingly. "I had to keep writing because I had to start the book all over."

"Has your writing improved?"

"Well, it had to, it couldn't get any worse."

"Do you think you'll keep writing?"

"Yes..." he said slowly "...but I don't understand why you're asking me these things."

"Well, why are you still writing?"

"Because...because...I, I have to..."

"If I had told you I didn't think your book was good, would you have continued to write?"

"I don't know," he studied me. "Probably not."

"That's why I lied to you."

"I don't understand."

"Jonathan, if you're someone who at twenty years old will spend months alone on a Greek island writing your memoirs, you obviously love to write. It's in you."

He stared at me.

"No one's first draft of their first book is any good. But you did it. You wrote it. And that's what real writers do, they write. I didn't want to cut you down. I didn't want to be the one to stop you. It's the months and the years that will make you a better writer. That's a huge part of it that you already have a handle on."

We both gazed out to the sea that had so inspired us for months at a time.

"I didn't enjoy lying to you, Jonathan, but the last thing I would ever want to do is discourage someone who's got half the battle licked. You're young, you have lots of time."

Now he was quiet, but he understood. Yeah, it was a drag. Yeah, he was now a little more grown up. But yeah, that's what it takes.

We hugged at that point, then sincerely wished each other luck.

I can't remember Jonathan's last name, but it wouldn't surprise me at all if he's a writer somewhere. Possibly a good one.

✴ ✴ ✴

"I never travel without my journal. One must always have something sensational to read on the train."

~ *Oscar Wilde*

LIBERAL AGENDA

This story was written originally in the third person and it's been kept that way...just because. It still belongs in this book.

It was a difficult time for Zazu. The feeling of living in a Sears store continued. LA, she decided, was one big Sears store. Maybe she should ride horses or have an affair, ride a ferris wheel at least, or return postcards to apologetic exes. Instead, she subscribed to the LA Times and followed Contra-gate, the political upheaval of the hour. In her spare time, she went to her job.

In two months of working at the flight desk at Santa Monica Airport forty-five hours a week, there had been no mention of Contra-gate, any Central American war, any other politics, art, children, nature, travel, philosophy, ideals, ideas, or even cooking, sewing, or sports. Cars, money, and partying were all her co-workers spoke of, with an occasional remark about sunglasses or beer. So, as far as Zazu could reason, at just thirty-six years old, the fun was over, and the most she could look forward to, maybe twenty years down the line and through bifocals, was counting wads of hundreds then stuffing them back under the t-shirts in her second drawer. Her current self had no schemes, and couldn't think of a way out. And it was cynical; all her inner voice ever said anymore was, "Yeah sure, buddy," or "Oh please, you idiot."

She was completely envious of Nancy, her plump little boss, who'd never been anywhere and was maybe twenty-three. Nancy sailed through any situation with total good cheer, getting what she needed on the way. Offending no one, Nancy got everyone to toe the line. Zazu wanted to ask Nancy if she tried to be like that or if she just was, but was afraid Nancy wouldn't know what she meant. Maybe everyone from Kansas was just solid, mild-mannered, determined, and industrious.

The others at work were a selection of kewpie dolls that, in the final analysis (or in the preliminary analysis), were the root of all the trouble. If these young girls were status quo, things were even worse than Zazu had surmised.

Two months earlier, standing at the end of the Santa Monica Pier, Zazu had asked the sky what on earth she should do next. The only novel undertaking she could come up with had been learning to fly. So, getting a job at the local airport as a flight dispatcher had seemed the logical intro into the world of small aircraft. But she didn't know that ninety percent of the pilots and the whole demographic that lives to fly got their wings in the military. Thus, left-leaning Zaz found herself on a job-site where Reagan worship was the overarching theme. Plus, she discovered that bumping through the clouds in Cessnas a) wasn't that thrilling, b) was more expensive than oceanfront acreage, and c) was essentially an ex-Air Force obsession.

What had led up to this term as a flight-dispatcher was a lengthy indulgence in travel, love, art, friendship, and restless searching. Zazu had believed these pursuits would ultimately lead to more of the same only better, and that she must continue following her instincts and the lines of her palm. But now she found these commitments more of a starvation diet. Overnight, things like new cars, credit cards, and accumulation had wiped out all the poetry and promise. Though yuppies had never seemed that smart, they had managed to pole-vault the flight-dispatcher stage where Zazu was grinding it out.

And she couldn't think up one more escape. Africa was still out there, and the Seychelles—some consolation—but somewhere between them and Zazu had to be some kind of…accumulation and construction. Clearly the only thing left to do, a cataclysmic adjustment, was to hoard greenbacks, stay in one place, and consider rescuing a cat.

She was also worried that the people at work would find out what the inside of her head was like and fire her.

It was a difficult time.

Meanwhile, Zazu was starting to miss all the people she'd alienated in her previous chapter. Not enough to forgive them, accept them, or even write to them, but at least she was starting to appreciate artists, eccentrics, siblings, fathers, and others who fail you when you're out of heart and out of pocket too many times in a row. She knew she'd have to revise her expectations and assumptions were she ever to mingle with them again, and she wasn't quite ready for that, but at least they could converse, worry about the world, and throw a sideways glance from time to time. It was weird throwing sideways glances alone.

Cards and letters from the English ex put her into a tail-spin. All Zazu truly wanted out of life, she explained to her friend Annette, was to look at beautiful land, beautiful cities, beautiful rooms and seas, to photograph them, protect them, do yoga in them, and to write about the juxtaposition of light, color, and social injustice. She wanted to ponder beauty, the rarity of it, and why so few promote and cherish it. She needed to preserve and cherish beauty. Still, she now planned to continue this airport stint for *two more years*, to prove to herself that money was everything.

Then the people at work found out what the inside of her head was like and fired her.

Zazu knew that God was getting back in touch with her and forgave Him instantly for aborting her two-year plan at only four and a half months.

After being fired, she suddenly found herself at the top of a ferris wheel. A good sign.

So Zazu decided that things had to be different now. Better. She was ready to come out of herself. She telephoned estranged relations and returned postcards. Reviewing her past, karmically and hygienically, she deduced she was not a likely target for Aids, and furthermore, a female in its prime should not be refrigerated but experiencing itself and its opposite to the fullest.

Tired of older, tall, handsome, spoiled filmmakers and the jigsaw of relationships, Zazu had stepped back for six months to reassess, and dispatch airplanes. Now she had a new idea about what she needed: a wholesome affair.

He would be cheerful, unattached, and busy. It would be easy to have a simple fling because men see affairs as the ultimate convenience—like a multi-vitamin. She would try it their way, since acting like a woman had so far seemed like a series of mistakes.

In a mere two weeks, a candidate drove into her vista—across her window frame to be exact—in his little white convertible. A man on a mission, he worked in the trendy office building next door. For months, Zazu had seen him zipping in and out of the parking lot. Sporting a buzz cut, he wore his unkempt Mercedes coupe like a pair of tennis shorts and seemed to scoot through life. Having never considered him before, suddenly he seemed just right: bouncy, younger, and short—something other than Zazu's exhausted ideal. He worked twelve-hour days and appeared to have no love interest in his little world. And little it was, from his five foot three lookout. "Perfect," decided Zazu.

But what sort of energetic enterprise was he conducting in that office of his? Representing the wrong side on toxic waste cases? Selling parcels of Amazon jungle to McDonald's? Zazu shied away from the office set because she found them too chatty about food and film.

Then he knocked on her door one morning, accompanied by a few `clients,' and Zazu learned, in her nightgown, that this `Freddy' was a realtor and selling the building she lived in. When he walked in, though, he just gazed around at the way she lived and the colors she liked, then looked into her eyes, nodded in recognition, and said, "Ohhh." Came in like an agent, went out like a fan.

Skating along the boardwalk one day, between weird gigs to earn a penny here, a dime there, Zazu rolled past Freddy sunning himself on a bench. He stopped her with a wave, and the next half hour revealed a surprisingly non-realtor profile. It turned out he was a justice lawyer who'd failed the bar twice and tumbled into real estate after discovering himself a brilliant car salesman. ("If I could sell cars that easily," he reasoned, "why not sell buildings?") In four years he planned to be out of real estate and back to law. Zazu raised a secret eyebrow, "Hmm, a leftie in disguise...." Justice, a nice thought. They talked about Nicaragua, and about the homeless droves swarming to the beach from all over the U.S., compliments of Reagan policies. But beyond his compassion, Zazu was taken with Freddy's very un-Californian ability to use three-syllable words. (He hailed from Ohio, of all places.) The icing on the cake, though, was his size; this would never be more than an affair, with Zazu towering five inches above him.

When Freddy asked her, a night or two later, to join him for a bite, her mind was made up. She had to be careful though. She didn't want Freddy to fall for her, didn't want trouble, just coziness. Just to thaw out and feel normal again. Kids and love and joint futures were behind her. She was a practical, working being who simply recognized that women and men need each other. This arrival at non-emotionality was an achievement.

Zazu and Freddy strolled around the sleepy seaside burg after dinner, crawling under fences to look at hidden patches of fabulous real estate she thought he should know about. And by 2 a.m., she'd led him to a secluded sofa on the upper balcony of a quiet bistro where they swilled red wine as the moon glowed upon the Pacific. Zazu feared the setting was too romantic and hoped Freddy wouldn't become ensnared by the ambience. And the later it got, the more it looked as if they were staying up because they liked each other.

In the ladies room, Zazu plotted her next move. Returning to Fred, adorable in his smallness on the couch, she giggled, "You know what I think?"

"What?"

"Never mind."

"What??"

"Well…I think…."

"What? Tell me."

"I can't."

"Don't get shy. Say it."

"Well…I was going to say that I think we should have an affair."

Freddy stared at her then raised his wine glass to his lips instead of speaking.

"I've never said that to anyone before," she confessed.

"I've never had it said to me before." He looked slightly nonplussed, though flattered.

"Well, what do you think?"

"Okay," Freddy smiled.

They sipped from their glasses another time, Zazu blushing at her naughtiness, Freddy studying his new paramour with curiosity. "May I kiss you?" he asked.

They kissed.

"Let's go," said Zazu.

Zazu felt good. Freddy was just the lover she wanted. Honest, local, and possessed by work. They knew all the same buildings. Having a male in her life was reassuring, and instead of judging his form like some art critic, she simply appreciated forgotten wonders such as hair on a chest, stubble on a face, and warm arms around her at night. Freddy told her he hadn't been with anyone for six months either, and seemed equally mesmerized by smooth legs and pointy hipbones.

Freddy was visibly affronted the first two times Zazu asked him not to touch her in public. Especially when public, to her, meant everywhere but her bedroom.

"You have a lot of rules, don't you...." he muttered, retracting the arm from her shoulders as they leaned on a fence in front of her apartment one night.

"It's just that I know a lot people in this town and I don't like them knowing my business. This ground-floor apartment is a fishbowl as it is. You know what I mean?"

"I guess so," said Freddy, but he down-shifted emotionally.

Zazu scored herself a point. Men were always so demonstrative in the first days, for the world to see. She felt these first days — while she was still adjusting to his height and realtor lingo — were hers, not the town's. She didn't even know what `escrow' meant yet. She felt successful in handling the affair her way, the man's way.

Freddy was now taking her to dinner or just appearing at her window every couple of nights. Zazu never asked about past loves, where he went when he wasn't with her, or when he was going to see her next. When he commented, several times, how he really wanted children, she said nothing. Surprising herself with her masculine ease, she considered making a lifestyle of this newly-found detachment.

Little Freddy was easy. As birth control, he practiced withdrawal, so no discussion was necessary there either. Until their third night together, when without warning he abandoned his method. Zazu had no idea how to be a man at a time like this…so she was quiet, but moved two inches away from him. She knew he expected a reaction, but knew better that the post-marathon slumber men are notorious for would engulf him momentarily, and it did. Left awake, as women are, she silently addressed her rage: "One false move by him and I'm saddled with a family? How dare he lure me into security then betray me? But why am I trusting a stranger in this most vulnerable area anyway? Classic female fool." She'd never have another abortion, that much she knew. And in some inarticulate way, she also knew that, at this point, anyone who got as far as her bedroom had passed some subtle fatherhood test—even over-zealous carrot-top realtors from Ohio. How could she tell this innocent man, who claimed he'd only been in love twice, what multiple abortions meant? She quietly wept into her pillow.

Freddy, born at 6 a.m., liked to repeat the experience daily. At the first whisper of light, he was already running late. He'd bolt at the first bird chirp, naked if Zazu didn't toss him his clothes. So if they were to discuss the, uh, incident, it would have to be pre-dawn. At 2 a.m., she nudged him, "Freddy?"

"Yeah?" He tried to make the `yeah' sound as if he hadn't been sleeping. Enterprising men like Freddy liked to believe they think all night.

"Wake up," Zazu said gently.

"Okay," he said breezily, no grogginess in his voice, "let me just go brush my teeth." He stumbled across the room. She couldn't not like him.

He returned to bed and snuggled in. "Is it really time to get up?" he was rubbing his eyes like a child. "It seems kinda early."

Zazu laughed. "It's only 2 o'clock. I just wanted to tell you that we have to get some condoms."

"Oh…yeah. I'll buy The Recycler in the morning."

Recycled condoms—Zazu laughed for about five minutes.

"What would you do if you got pregnant?" he asked her then.

Zazu knew she would have the baby. But she didn't want to seem like the eternal woman-who-wants-to-have-a-baby. She didn't want to lie though, misrepresent herself, or even talk about this till she knew this man a lot better. Freddy awaited her reply.

"I'd…………flip," was the simplest true answer she could muster.

"I really want to have children," Freddy said for the fourth time since they met.

"Well, that's obvious," said Zazu.

Just as Zazu was keeping score, so was Freddy. But on his scorecard, aloof detachment did not earn good marks. And when Zazu off-handedly mentioned a current husband, she garnered another demerit.

"You didn't tell me you were married," he said stiffly.

"It's really not…like that," she brushed it off, again not wanting to read aloud Chapter 99 of `My Unruly Life.'

Freddy never probed further about this hubby — where he was, who he was, what had happened — and Zazu was glad.

One dawn, two weeks into the liaison that Zazu was beginning to enjoy, Freddy told her that he didn't like having a casual affair, that although it was fun at first, he wanted to be in love. Casual sex was not for him.

Did he like her too much, she wondered, or not enough? It was tough to believe that in all the world she'd managed to find the one man who didn't like casual sex.

"When I said `Let's have an affair,'" she said to Fred, who was sitting seriously on the edge of the bed she was still in, "I didn't say `Let's have a meaningless affair.'"

"I know," said Freddy slowly, "but maybe we should just leave it…you know…and be friends…and……see what happens. You know?"

She didn't know at all. "Yeah," she said.

"Because, I don't know, I just don't feel right about this," he said. "I wanna be in love."

"I don't wanna be in love," Zazu said firmly. "I don't want to fall in love, that's for sure. I don't believe in that anymore because all it means is that you're madly in love and gonzo for awhile, and then it wears off and you're right back to square one. Why bother?"

"I know what you mean. And I agree when you put it like that…. I guess I don't want to *fall* in love either…."

"I would like to just like somebody," Zazu said, "then like them some more, and then some more. That would be nice."

"Yeah," Freddy agreed dreamily. He walked over to the window.

"I'd just like to avoid the emotional side," said Zazu.

"You can't," said Freddy. "You never can."

They were silent as he put on his sneakers.

Zazu knew his two big dogs were waiting at home for their morning run on the beach.

"So…should we call it off?" she needed to ask before he left.

"No…." Freddy's voice trailed off as if there was lots more to say but he wasn't going to say any of it. "Can we just be light about it?"

"Yeah," she agreed. (She could hardly say, "No, let's be heavy.")

"I still want you to work for me, though," he said gingerly, as if he may have offended her. He'd asked her to photograph every building in the town for him so he could create a photo file system for his business. Freddy had huge visions. "I'm very serious about that project. Will you still do it?"

"Yes," she said, needing the money.

So, as the affair screeched to a halt, triggered by Zazu knew not what, she had to report to Freddy's adjacent office each morning.

It was nice to see him every day—she liked his pink t-shirts and khaki shorts—but it was awkward. Just as they'd been getting closer, to the point where Zazu no longer recoiled if he touched her in public, suddenly they were boss and worker. And since Freddy did the work of six men, making literally one hundred phone calls a day and selling buildings hand over fist, the atmosphere was less than romantic. Zazu tried to be polite and a good employee, but secretly waited for traces of endearment. The day she left a flower on his desk, he kissed her in the parking lot, but nothing else transpired.

After two weeks, Freddy encountered a financial set-back due to inexperience (and sushi bars). He couldn't pay his secretary, his creditors, or Zazu. Not knowing when he'd be back in the chips, Zazu was forced to quit and find other work. Freddy resented it, and resented the bill she sent for two weeks of her time. No photos had been taken since Freddy had no money for film, but Zazu had dutifully reported to work every morning and waited around for hours until he was again sure no money was coming in that day.

"Did you quit because you didn't get paid?" asked her friend, Annette.

"No," said Zazu, "I quit because I didn't get laid."

Had Zazu fallen for him? Neither she nor her friends could comprehend how a one-month romp with someone selected for the convenience factor had made a wimp out of her while four and a half months at the airport had made her a trooper.

But Zazu knew why she'd become fond of Freddy. The little things he'd said—like when someone had approached them on the boardwalk about religion, and she'd said, "I'm a Taoist," (hoping to discourage the impending Jesus rap), Freddy had chirped, "I am, too," surprising both Zazu and the Christian, who fled. She thought it was cute that he was always hungry for artichokes (they were always gentle on his mind), and that he knew the composers of classical music pieces. Freddy knew lots of things. Another time, when she was sitting in his office, he'd ended a sentence with, "…and you should probably get your real estate license—you'd be great at this." He didn't look at her or wait for a response, but continued, sort of talking to the floor as he dialed call number eighty-seven, "No, you wouldn't feel right about it."

And that first day they'd spoken, when he'd been sunbathing on the bench and she had skated by, he'd hurdled all small talk with the question, "What do you want to do that you haven't done yet?" And when she'd listed her ambitions—to travel to Japan, Australia, and Africa; to have a photo exhibit in LA; and to live in New Mexico again and write a novel—he'd matter-of-factly replied, "Sounds like you need me."

But that was then, and at the time she'd pretended not to hear that generous remark. Now she wondered where he got the nerve to talk that way. She was hurt, and regretted everything she'd revealed.

After some pensive bike rides, Zazu got a few journalist assignments going again. She drew the blinds. It was dark in her little flat but at least she didn't have to watch the red-haired annoyance zig-zag from office door to Mercedes and back all day. Getting in and out of his car was clearly his preferred exercise, explaining the premature paunch.

"What do you see in him?" shrugged Annette.

"We're just alike," said Zazu, confusing her friend altogether. "I mean, you know that big house on Pacific Avenue that they just painted dark turquoise?"

"You mean the one where they painted their picket fence that color, too?"

"Yeah. Well, the other day me and Freddy were driving by it and I asked him what he thought of the paint job. And he said, `It's so awful that I kinda like it.' And that's exactly how I feel."

"Do his feet touch the floor when he sits at his desk?" Annette wanted to know, "or does he swing them?"

"That's mean," said Zazu.

Annette was still into older, tall, handsome, spoiled ego-maniacs. "You're gonna look back at this obsession and really wonder about yourself someday," she sighed.

"That's what everybody says."

"He's a jerk."

"I just feel something between us. I think he cares."

"Move on. He's just a control freak with two big dogs. I know it's hard to get over a guy with great dogs. It took me two years to forget a guy's dog—but do it."

Zazu longed for Freddy. Was he secretly pining away for her appeal and detachment but too proud? Or did he despise her and dread the sight of both her and her windows? She elected to phone him at home one evening, for the facts.

"Freddy, it's Zazu."

"Are you calling about the bill?" he asked coldly.

"No……I'm—"

"I DON'T want to talk about the bill."

"I'm not calling about that…. I thought maybe I'd hop on my bike and come and talk to you. I don't like the phone much."

"Well, what is it you want to say?" Freddy liked the phone fine.

"Well…I was just thinking that maybe you don't trust me very much."

"Of course I trust you. Why would you say a thing like that? I mean one of the very first conversations we had was about the problems in Nicaragua, how could I not trust you?"

"I thought maybe you don't trust me because of the way I initiated our…affair. Maybe you thought I was aloof."

"What do you mean?"

"I don't know…I thought maybe you thought I was being insensitive."

"No, not really…."

"Because I thought it was weird the way we suddenly stopped being lovers and started working together a few days later," said Zazu. "I felt funny about the whole thing."

"Well," he said, "we never did get to work together really, and…and…we never really— Neither relationship really took off."

"Well, you ended it," she said.

"Yeah, well, like I told you, for me it's ALL or NOTHING. I'm not in a position to have a relationship right now. I don't want it. What I really need right now is a friend. That's what I need. A friend. Not a lover. And that's the only way I can get to know somebody. You know, take some time, be friends, and maybe kiss once in a while. Like that."

"That's a bit programmed, isn't it?" said Zazu quietly.

"That's the way I am. I've only been with a few women, you know. And our little affair was starting to be too…I don't know. But you'll remember that it started out to be just an affair, with no strings attached. Those were practically your words. But it was getting too intense for me. I don't have the time for that right now."

"Well, I liked our affair," said Zazu. "I thought it was just fine. In fact, I think we should have another one."

Freddy chuckled.

"I just wanted you to know," she went on, "that I wasn't being cold when I indicated that I just wanted an affair; I was being careful."

"At my expense," said Freddy.

"Well, I learned my lesson," said Zazu. "I'll never ask a man to have an affair again."

Freddy chuckled again, then conceded a little. "I admit it felt great. But with me it's really all or nothing. That's just the way I am. I'm a loner. It's what I have to do right now. I'm so involved in my work, I never even see my dogs anymore."

"They're never home?"

Freddy giggled, "No, they're never around anymore."

✳ ✳ ✳

Moral of the story: Predators, don't expect your prey to love you.

THE ART OF PLACEMENT

5 illustrations

1. Birthday Presence

Each year, I give myself a birthday present. It might be something as simple as a real day off or it might be fancier. Usually in May or June I'll scour my psyche for unrealised desires. Something I might be yearning for, missing, or neglecting. In 2006, the gift was to hike the full length of a beautiful coastal path I had never completed.

On the appointed day, I set out bright and early with Rosie the Wonder Dog. The weather was made-to-order and we both felt spunky hitting the trail. Traveling light, we had everything we'd need for three or four hours. Hugging the coast, this path took in stony overlooks and wound down to isolated coves. And, by leaving early, we probably wouldn't see anyone else at all.

In Hawai'i, many locals hike in flip-flops, or `slippahs' as they're fondly known. It's hard to explain why, we're all just hooked on them, to the extent that wearing anything else feels like bondage. But they keep our feet cool, they go easily on and off at home or at the beach, they're light and easy to hose off later, they're inexpensive, and...you get the idea.

As Rosie and I clambered down our first hill toward the mini-waterfall where we'd take a soak, it struck me I'd forgotten to pack a pair of back-up slippahs. The ones I was wearing, a solid pair of Reefs with decent tread, weren't exactly new. And the one shortcoming of hiking in flip-flops is that if one should break, you have to finish the hike half barefoot. Considering the rocks, smaller stones, mud, heat, dirt, and distance, it won't be a trail or tale with a happy ending.

My odds of breaking a shoe were only around 10%, but the stupidity factor bugged me. How hard is it to throw another pair of weightless rubber thongs into a backpack? And I'd even remembered...until I forgot.

With this nagging thought, my slippahs seemed to look more beat up and ready to give every time I glanced down. Should we not hike quite as far as planned? But the trail was tugging us onward. It was a perfect morning, and Rosie was as delirious as I to be out there.

The first hour went as swimmingly as expected. Each fresh cove we stumbled upon was lovely in its own way. An hour along, we reached an overlook above a small, idyllic beach with azure waters. I decided to hydrate Rosie, snack on an orange, then perch on the ground up there amongst some small boulders and do a meditation. There might not be a more divine spot.

Rosie welcomed a break in the shade, so we took a load off. I scanned the immediate vicinity for a suitable place to settle on the ground. I can still recall the cleanliness of the earth there and the blue goodness of the ocean and sky. It was everything summer could be, Rosie was smiling by my side and...it was my birthday. I closed my eyes and let the

All and Everything sweep over and through me. I gave thanks for my life thus far, for this day, this island, this friend, and these blessings.

After twenty minutes or so, we were ready to resume the path. But as I turned to reach for my backpack, I observed something on the ground just a couple of feet away: another pair of rubber flip-flops. Not one junky, broken sandal, as one normally finds out on trails—that lone, orphaned shoe we've all seen a million times—but a neatly placed pair. Probably previously worn by a man, they were neither new nor a custom fit, but they were intact and wearable. And clearly they were abandoned since there wasn't a soul visible on land or sea. So here was the final thing (or two things) needed to make my day.

I accepted the gift, placed the slippahs in my backpack, and off we marched, now really without a care. And, no, I didn't need to employ them, but the affirmation served me well.

2. I Got Your Back

Not long after becoming licensed for massage in LA, I happened upon a little wooden plant stand in an IKEA store. Extremely light, this unique item might make a good massage stool since it folded flat and would fit into the pouch of my table's carrying case. And once in Hawai'i, where out-call massage sustained me from day one, this little `chair' became an essential tool. When working in resorts, I never had to drag armchairs across the room, as I watched other massage therapists doing.

The top of the stool was constructed of thin wooden strips about an inch wide. And it was disconcerting one day when one of these came loose. Though I had a carpenter friend reinforce it, soon another of the strips actually snapped in two. Customized carpentry, in this case, wouldn't be at all cost effective now. Plus, another strip could snap at any time. What to do?

Buy another chair.

But there was no IKEA in all of Hawai'i. Besides, the rest of the chair was fine, just a bit unsightly now with that one slat missing.

Then another slat snapped. Now the chair was looking shabby. I knew I couldn't keep repairing it. Damn! It was the best little portable massage chair.

This was one of those concerns too trivial to qualify as a problem, yet demanding attention. I wanted to simply buy a new stool next time I went to the Mainland for holidays, but there was no IKEA in my hometown either.

One Kaua'i morning, Rosie and I went for a swim at our secret spot. Having found a new footpath to this secluded beach, we parked on the shoulder of the quiet lane. Later, satiated from sun and swimming, we returned to the car. Opening the passenger door on the grassy side to let Rosie hop in, I stepped on something half buried in the ground — a junky wooden thing. But it caught my attention and I leaned down for a look. Picking it up, I found myself holding the top portion of an IKEA plant stand, identical to mine. It was only the top piece with the wooden slats. A couple were missing, but most were in place.

I found it extraordinary and uncanny that the sole person on the island (or in the world) who needed this precise wooden construction, should haphazardly park so close to it that I stepped on it. Moreover, no one else who even stooped to pick it up out of sheer curiosity would ever have known what on earth it was.

Needless to say, I nabbed it. And to this day, seventeen years into my bodywork career, I still use my original IKEA stool, and every now and then, when one of the wooden slats happens to break, I've got back up.

3. Eekosi

In the Greek alphabet, there's no `W'. So, if you're in Greece and your name starts with a `W' (take `Wendy' as a casual example), the Greeks aren't sure how to say it. This happened to me a lot there. Yanni, Yorgo, Eleni, and Dimitri couldn't pronounce `Wendy' because `W' was a foreign sound.

The closest they would come was always "Gwendy" or "Oo-endy," and they knew they weren't nailing it. And it was hard for me to say, "Yeah, you got it," when their pronunciation sounded really weird. But there were other English words many Greeks did know, particularly the numbers, since many of them did business with tourists. So, not infrequently, when trying to say my name, a Greek might try "Twenty?" Then, of course, we'd both laugh—who would have a name like that?

But, since this was the easiest for the Greeks, who I adored befriending, eventually `Twenty' became my name. And, sometimes, especially when meeting someone who knew no English at all, I'd suggest the Greek word for `twenty': `*eekosi*.' That, too, brought laughter, "Your name is *Eekosi*?" Having a number for a name was even more unlikely in Greek than English, because the Greeks primarily use traditional names of saints and biblical entities. `*Eekosi*' is not one of them, no Saint Twenty.

But I'd actually always thought it would be fun having a number for a name—you could sign off with a digit. And, as it happened, my Greek nickname followed me back to London and the U.S., where I had Greek friends.

Fast forward five years. I'm now acting, modeling, and writing in Los Angeles (though forever a Greek Islander under the glad-rags). Knowing I'm late to Hollywood at age twenty-seven, I'm in do-or-die mode, determined to succeed, and living on whole wheat toast, oatmeal, and popcorn while waiting for the next audition, call-back, or go-see.

And though the jobs that trickled in actually paid fairly well, life always cost just a little more, so it was a lean time. Luckily, in 1978 a dollar went farther than twenty dollars now, but I was basically living on salt air and Fritos, and young enough to do so. Though it wasn't stylish to be broke, it was neither shockingly unusual nor badly frowned upon; young adults were granted more experimental latitude back then. And, in the most free-spirited generation in the history of western civilization, I was hardly the only starving artist.

But empty pockets take their toll. I remember my hesitation in calling a friend to see if he could pay me back the five dollars I'd lent him two months ago.

My inseparable friend, Esmé, lived across the hall. While dating bad boys and figuring out our twenties, we'd roller-skate and body-surf to burn off our angst. Less willing to `suffer' than I, Esmé gravitated toward more lucrative pursuits like production work and location scouting. She could forego being the artiste in order to eat regular food.

Though we lived right at the beach, I couldn't afford furniture, so my bed was not only a piece of foam on the floor, but a slim piece. My night table was a cardboard box concealed under a flowery Greek scarf. And the prize acquisition was a loaned wooden table from a neighbor, at which I could work on my book when not making Hollywood rounds.

On Easter Sunday, I woke to a crisp blue sky and rays of golden sun. Rolling out of bed (easily done when your bed is one inch high), I went to the bathroom. Ruminating there about whether to make toast or oatmeal, I instead decided to crawl back to bed — it was a holiday.

But, approaching my bed, I couldn't overlook something neatly displayed upon one of my two white pillows: a twenty-dollar bill.

Of course I was elated to find any amount of unexpected cash in my marginal life—and, it was clearly intended for me since no one else lived there and it was on my pillow—but…where did it come from? The Tooth Fairy?

Before even plucking it from the pillow, I regarded the window over the bed. Did it blow in somehow?

The window was closed. Anyway, wouldn't I have seen it a few minutes ago when I woke up? Right now, for all intents and purposes, it appeared to have been magically placed there while I was in the bathroom.

The Easter Bunny?

No, Esmé had done it. Her father was a pastor, and she must've felt some Christian calling to help out her penniless pal on this holy day. She lived right across the hall and even had keys to my place.

But how could Esmé know the exact moment I awoke and went into the bathroom? Or did she sneak in during the night, and I had overlooked the money when I first woke up? Once up and dressed, I'd knock on her door. It had to be Esmé, there was no other explanation. And she was a generous and kindly soul. (Though not a magician.)

The great news was I now had twenty bucks. And my name was Twenty. Plus it was Easter. This was personal and much appreciated.

But a while later, Esmé feigned total ignorance about the event. Not only did she say she didn't put it there, but she convinced me. How could she have possibly silently slipped into my apartment at that precise moment, she asked. Or during the night without me waking up. "I wish I could say I did," she said, "it would've been a nice thing to do. But no, I didn't have anything to do with it."

I made her swear on a stack of Bibles. A pastor's kid wouldn't do that if it was a lie.

And so went the fairytale. No one else had the keys to my apartment. And several more times over the following weeks (even years), I revisited the incident with Esmé — she really didn't put that money there.

4. The Spiritual Take

Sylvia, a British medium in London, connected me to my mother's spirit when I was twenty-one. She did so with such panache that I remained moved by it ever thereafter.

She assured me that, going forward, my mother would be accessible to me — I just needed to call on her. But, like anything, communing with spirits takes practice. And, once out of Sylvia's graces, I didn't feel as connected.

One of my only keepsakes from my mother was a silver chain necklace I loved and wore. I'd been wearing it three years when, one day as I was walking out the front door, I felt it sliding down my chest — the clasp had broken.

Relieved not to have lost it, I brought it back upstairs. Holding it in my hand, and thinking about my mother, I got the idea to offer it back to her as a test. How real was her spirit? I understood that the point of spiritual communion isn't to tell ghosts what to do, to interrogate them, or expect human behavior, but giving credence to the invisible was new to me, and I wanted confirmation. "Mom," I said, "if you really are present in the spiritual form, take this necklace back. Then I'll know for sure."

I had to conceal it somewhere she'd have easy access to. I looked around my bedroom for a discreet spot. The door was in a corner, and between it and the wall was a space of maybe an inch and a half. In that crevice was a tiny nail stuck in the doorjamb. "I'll put the necklace right here," I said out loud, placing its end loop on the nail, so the slim chain hung down the door-frame, invisible to anyone. Even Zeke, my lover and roommate, wouldn't see it there. "Okay," I said, "take it, Mom."

I gave her some lead-time to reclaim it, and was surprised when I checked about a week later and the necklace was still hanging there. "It's still here for you, Mom, right here," I pointed to it.

I gave her more time. Who knew what her `schedule' was like up there? But, again, after another week or two, the necklace remained undisturbed in the space between the door and the wall. I wasn't disappointed since I knew Mom's compliance was a long shot, but neither was I convinced I'd have a lot more communication with my newly-acquired angel.

After a few weeks, I stopped expecting the necklace to vanish, since it never did. And, about two months later, I actually forgot about it as I made a decision to move back to the States. And, in packing up all my stuff, the necklace was completely overlooked in its hiding place.

Zeke had plans to join me in New York several months later. After I left London, we were constantly on the phone and writing letters. So, when I realized I'd left my precious necklace, I told him where it was and asked him to take it down and bring it to me when he flew over. (He'd seen me always wearing it before it broke, and knew exactly what to look for.)

But the next time we spoke, he said he found the little nail but there was nothing on it.

"You must've looked in the wrong place," I said, and described more precisely where the nail was in the doorjamb.

Next time we spoke, Zeke assured me he'd found the right nail, but again there was no necklace on it.

I knew I hadn't removed the necklace myself. But it had seemed apparent that my mother didn't want it back. (Probably not much occasion for jewelry in her new stomping grounds.) So I begged Zeke to search everywhere in the room. Maybe it fell off the hook. It had to be there somewhere. I never explained why I'd left it on that nail, just said it was for safekeeping until I got it fixed. But Zeke knew the sentimental value the necklace held for me and promised to find it.

When next we spoke, he said he'd searched the entire room and couldn't find it anywhere. Now I was getting nervous because once Zeke left London, neither of us would be returning to that flat. But soon, Zeke, too, was packing for New York. "Please, please find the necklace — this is the last chance," I implored him.

But after packing, and even scouring every square inch of the room, Zeke reported that the necklace simply wasn't there.

5. Who Knew?

I was twenty-one, it was early spring, I didn't really live anywhere, had just spent the winter in Albuquerque, and didn't know where I wanted to go next. Not home to Eastern Long Island. Maybe up to Nova Scotia where my brother, Sonny, was dodging the draft in a log cabin he'd built, and where my sister, Mimi, had recently joined him. Not ecstatic about going north in spring, I was still quite curious about Nova Scotia, and their rustic lifestyle sounded appealing.

So, after driving east from New Mexico, my boyfriend dropped me in New York City. I'd say hi to my granny, spend a night or two, then hitch-hike up to Canada. To avoid thumbing out of New York City madness, instead I took the train out to the North Fork of Long Island, from whence I'd grab the ferry to Rhode Island. From there I could start hitching to Nova Scotia. It would take a couple of days.

Though my father, step-mother, and siblings were on the South Fork of Long Island, to go there would be off course. When hitching, every day and every dollar count. Plus, the step-situation was awkward; I'd give it a pass.

So I took the train to the east end of the North Fork. And, according to the ferry schedule, I'd have sufficient time to get from the train station to the dock. Once off the train, I had to walk through the town to the road leading to the ferry. Ambling down Main Street — not a place South Fork people ever went since that required two additional, pricey ferries to get there — who should drive by at that precise moment but my father and step-mother? Going the opposite direction, they didn't see me (nor expect to, believing I was in New Mexico).

I could afford ten minutes to say hello. They appeared to be on their way to line up for their own ferry a few blocks away. So I did a one-eighty and ran, clumsily with the baggage, in hopes of catching them before they boarded their boat.

Panting up to the dock, I spotted their VW camper idling in the line. Taking them completely by surprise, I tapped on my dad's window. "Hi Dad!"

"What're you doing here?" he rolled down the window.

"We thought you were in New Mexico," said my step-mother, Darlene.

"I was, but I'm on my way to Nova Scotia now."

"Oh, you are?" Dad seemed interested. "What're you gonna do there?"

"Gonna visit Sonny and Mimi."

"You better hop in and come with us instead," he said paternally.

"Really? Why?"

"There's something you should see on the South Fork."

"Really? What?" What it could be? What would justify a u-turn right now?

"Sonny and Mimi," said Dad. "They came home two days ago."

So divine or parental intervention spared me a long, fruitless trip. And, even if just by `coincidence,' it's reassuring to have one's compass recalibrated by a well-placed parent.

I hopped in the camper and went home.

✳ ✳ ✳

STARVING ARTIST

I didn't even realize until my mid-forties what `starving artist' actually meant; I thought the `starving' part referred to one's passion, like fasting for a cause. Creativity trumped your physical needs. `Starving artist,' I thought, was an emotional preference—like you'd rather do your art than eat. Like dying for love or something.

Anyway, I was skinny but I wasn't starving. Oatmeal for breakfast, popcorn for dinner. I had my 1968 Dodge Dart (the unsexiest car ever made, yet one of the best) to power me on and off the freeways. And the soundtrack was Randy Newman singing, "We Love LA." Esmé and I had our adjacent apartments on Venice Beach, and the `poverty' I'd chosen was more a calculated risk.

It was about priorities. You either committed to solvency and getting ahead or to the artist's life. If you put your time and energy into acting, you probably wouldn't have a new car. If you put your time and energy into acquiring cars and houses, you wouldn't be available for auditions or acting jobs. One or the other. Everybody knows about the artist syndrome. And everybody has the choice to dance or paint or play guitar on a subway platform instead of going to the office.

And there was even a time when I called into question the value of art and artists. Does society really need any of it? Or is all of it a great big indulgence? Then I spent time in Nicaragua during the Contra War, where there was no art at all anywhere. (Art and war don't co-exist.) And that's when art and artists were fully validated for me. Without art, life was colorless and flat. Without gardens and flowers, without pretty dresses, without music, decorations on walls, without books and stories, without theater, dance, movies, cool haircuts, and even shell anklets, a great empty space truly aches for it all.

So, it's not a bad thing to play out one's youth and illusions, banking on time and innocence. As long as we get real in time to survive. And one day, at age forty-four, I suddenly went, "Oh-h, starving artist—like no money for food. Starving as in hungry. Oh-h-h." And suddenly art took a back seat to the game of catch-up I was going to have to start playing pretty hard.

But that was later. Right now I was a twenty-eight-year-old actress in LA, and advancing my career consumed my calendar. I had a part in a Tennessee Williams play. And that the small theater was only blocks from my apartment was a plus.

Venice Beach was seedy back in the day, if not dangerous. The boardwalk was deserted at night except for ne'er-do-wells. And this theater was in an old rarely-used beachside arena. Who knew what else went on by that secluded building late at night? So, despite the proximity, I'd drive to rehearsals and park right close to the building.

It was after 10:00 when we finished rehearsing one night, and upon pulling away, I was stopped by a police car. The cop approached my window, "Why were you parked over there?"

"I was rehearsing for a play," I said.

"Do you know you're missing a tail light?"

"I am?"

"Yes, you are."

"Is that illegal?"

"Yes, it is."

"Oh, I'm sorry. I'll get it fixed."

"Just stay right there and I'll be back," he instructed, and walked back to his car. I sat in the dark bemoaning my fate.

The officer soon returned and said, "Are you aware that you have an outstanding unpaid ticket for an illegal u-turn on Robertson Boulevard?"

Oh, God. "I am aware, but I haven't been able to pay it yet."

"Well, it's going to have to be paid."

"When do I have to pay it by?"

"Tonight."

"Right now?? I don't have any money on me."

"Not right this minute, but you'll have to come to the police station tonight and pay it. According to the records, and including the late penalty, you owe sixty dollars for that ticket."

"What should I do?"

"Do you live near here?"

"Yes."

"You have some money at home?"

"I have a little, but maybe not enough. Or my friend might be able to lend me some."

"Okay," said the cop, "let's go to your place."

"You're coming with me?"

"Myself and my partner," he nodded toward the car where accusing lights continued flashing. "We'll follow you."

Who knew illegal u-turns were so hardcore? With my police escort, I drove the few blocks to my place, where all three of us then went upstairs and entered my humble abode. The two uniformed authorities with their guns and big black shoes dominated the space almost comically (almost) as I internally debated whether to surrender my last few bucks (I had exactly sixty) or to inquire about my options. Sadly, Esmé wasn't home to front me some cash.

"I only have sixty dollars to my name right now," I told the fuzz, who found this plausible in light of the non-existent furnishings. "I don't think I should part with all of it."

"Well, what are you gonna do?"

"What are my options?" Maybe they'd settle for half now and half at the turn of the century.

"You can spend a night in jail…."

"Can't I just pay this a little later?"

"It already is a little later and you haven't paid it."

"One night in jail?"

"One night should do it." They passed each other a straight-faced cop-glance with amused eyes.

"And then the ticket will be absolved?"

"Spending a night in jail should ameliorate the fine."

I then offered them my two wrists pressed together, ready for cuffing, "Take me away."

Now they both smiled. "We won't need to handcuff you," one said. "You're compliant."

If one night in the clink would wipe out the ticket, it seemed worth it. Not exactly what I'd planned this evening, but I was mildly curious about prison anyway, and it had never seemed accessible before.

We didn't simply cruise over to the local lock-up, though. The boys in blue drove way out into the San

Fernando Valley, with me in the back seat, secured behind the grill. Apparently, late at night, all the evil-doers were pooled in one central holding tank. And when we arrived, it was clear that the night's work was just beginning over there.

Thus, I was deposited and `processed.' It was kind of like Las Vegas, in that way that the real world drops away and you're inside now. What's happening in here has no relevance to anything elsewhere — a world entirely its own.

What I instantly discovered, and what continued to be driven home throughout my stay, was that your identity vaporizes the moment you step into confinement. Not only does it not matter who you are or what you might have to say, but no one believes you anyway. This is jail, sweetheart, no one can be trusted, no one necessarily tells the truth, and prisoners have no say in anything. You're a prisoner, sweetheart.

The whole u-turn thing and missing tail-light were never mentioned again — no one cared why I was there, I was just there. And there I'd stay. It didn't matter if I was hungry, thirsty, tired, old, young, rich, poor, horrible, or a goody two-shoes, I was now one more female in a container full of them. My twelve or fourteen cellmates in this slammer — who were all already there when I arrived and spoke occasionally to each other but not to me — seemed more like one disconcerted herd of prostitutes or drug-dealers, as if they'd been corralled and hauled in en masse. They also seemed less flabbergasted than me to be there.

It wasn't scary or vile or creepy, but your standard jail format with rows of bunk-beds and one seatless toilet in a corner for all to view. Unsympathetic wardens and/or administrative types occasionally passed our cell, but had little or no interaction with us. There may have been one or two fresh felons plunked into the pen during the night, but the joint was otherwise void of big drama.

It wasn't restful though. We were each given a skimpy cover and stingy `pillow' (bag of gravel), but the fluorescent lights remained on, the workers and their phones stayed active just outside the bars, and not one of my new pier group was enthralled with these new digs. There was mumbling, even shouting, as the girls grappled with these sudden circumstances, some probably needing substances they were now deprived of, one pregnant one begging for milk. No, it wasn't a nice break from the workaday world, it was a big mess. But I'd be out in the morning.

Morning—a continuation of the noisy, sleepless angst—began at 5:30 a.m. when we were each handed a cardboard breakfast. Having clearly been through the flavor-extractor, it was as you'd imagine—not gray, but it tasted gray. I couldn't eat it. But I'd be out soon.

From 5:30, we were officially up—though no one had slept a wink—and the morning trudged along with nothing happening whatsoever. Around 6 or 7, I flagged down a passing county employee to find out when I'd be released. She said she didn't know anything about it and I'd be handled as my paperwork dictated. Clearly, discussing things wasn't the protocol around here. As far as this worker was concerned, I was a serial killer. A second probe about my release was equally unsuccessful, and it was even insinuated that I was getting rowdy and might end up in solitary. The other damsels in distress had a better handle on inmate etiquette and the sequence of events (or non-events). But I had stuff to do—I needed to get outta here! It was now 10:00!

Around 11:00, there were some stirrings, buzz that we might be leaving. Whew.

But, again, given no info, we were all summarily guarded into a van, seated in rows, and taken on a long drive......to another jail. By now it was 1 p.m., I was being booked into a bigger facility, and no one in my outside world even knew my whereabouts. At this second house of confinement, I grew concerned.

Here, they just had us sit on benches against a wall for a number of hours. I was somehow able to beg for a couple of phone calls, but could only reach the answering services of friends. "Help, I'm in jail," was all I could convey, since I knew not where I was or whence I'd be freed. But I did reach one friend who I implored to please track down Esmé for me.

As we all waited, two or three of my sisters in sin divulged their infractions. One young woman had been arrested for mopin'. `With intent to sell' might've been the sub-infraction, or `mopin' under the influence.' But the actual charge was `moping' and had to do with a certain high-profile park bench in South Central where moping was apparently a career choice for some. There was also a jay-walker. Maybe jay-running from the cops? This miss confessed that, once relegated to the back of the squad car, she off-loaded her cocaine into the crease between the top and bottom vinyl seats. And I suppose my fellow outlaws wondered what the sub-crime of my `illegal u-turn' might be. `With intent to go the other direction?'

I managed eventually to get a word with a lesser prison guard. "I was supposed to be released this morning," I told her.

"I don't think so," she replied.

"But I was only supposed to be in for one night."

"Well, nobody gets released from this facility," she said. "This is basically a way station."

"What do you mean?"

"Everybody here is going to Sybil Brand."

"What's civil brand?"

"Sybil Brand County Jail," she enunciated.

"Oh, no."

She raised her eyebrows and shrugged. "Maybe see what you can do once you get over there."

Things weren't going as planned. (And no lunch was served.)

Around 4:00, we gals were gathered again, to be unceremoniously conducted to the Big House. More heavily guarded now, we were prodded onto a bus this time—like, a Department of Corrections bus plastered in signage, the type chain gangs commute in, hardly what you want to be spotted in by your agent on the 405 Freeway.

Sybil Brand was one of those foreboding, 1950's-style, super-grim edifices that reek and ooze of misery. Just seeing a photo of the place is enough to keep most Southern Californians properly behaving for life. You don't want to go to Sybil Brand. Nor did I. I'd never even heard of it until an hour ago. (And I even felt sorry for the original Sybil—surely a well-intentioned philanthropist, but dumb idea to have a penitentiary named after you.) Anyway, I was now aboard a bus bound for just that happy place. Moreover, I appeared to have an indeterminate sentence; nowhere did it seem recorded why I was here or for what duration. I was being clandestinely digested in the foul bowels of the LA penal system, never to be seen again.

On the eastern fringe of downtown Los Angeles, our ride rumbled in close to the back door of the imposing Sybil Brand Institute. And I'm here to tell you, this is NOT a place you want your bus to drop you off. Picture the hugest, worst-looking building you've ever seen. "Oh well, this is good material," I appeased myself.

We filed in, accustomed now to non-entity status, and were clinically processed, this time stripped of our own clothing and given striped outfits. But we could only don the zebra-wear after getting deloused, hosed down, and inspected. They don't fool around in county jail.

That was sobering. I put on my striped pj's and was led to my cell. (You better believe I'd be thinking twice about future u-turns.) It was a long hike to my cell-block. Sybil Brand was massive and not exactly scenic inside. A nauseous green pallor, cast by the weak lighting, made the endless hallways indistinguishable from one another. Just floor upon floor, row upon row, of barred cells housing over two thousand convicts in striped suits, some spending years there, some decades. And there was a distinct smell, I'm sure unique to penitentiaries—the smell of time standing still mixed with harsh sanitizers, stale humans, and no oxygen.

And I was privileged—I didn't know when, but I was still relatively certain I'd be exiting this theme park without too much wear on my soul.

In the meantime, I was delivered to my cell where I met my new life companion. She seemed okay. Had been there a while. May have been disappointed my infringement was so lackluster. Probably thought my u-turn story was a cover for something grisly. Illegal u-turn, yeah, that's what they all say. Illegal u-turn with a body in the trunk? This is Sybil Brand, we're not here for moving violations.

Inside our modest pen were two slim bunk-beds, a sink, and a toilet. I was told we were free to exit this cubicle and walk along the cell-block (consisting of about five other units), but that was about it.

I figured we two would have ample time to get acquainted (years), and didn't want her to fear she'd been further punished with a chatterbox underachiever, so I walked down the cell-block and waited inside the bars for an authority to pass. As soon as one did, I earnestly pleaded how I believed there'd been a mistake and that I needed someone to follow up on my case. It was now 7 p.m. (And dinner was not served.)

I then went back to my little cell, and for the first time in what felt like days, I relaxed my body and mind. At least this cage was mine—all the restless mopers and jay-walkers who'd surrounded me all night and all day were somewhere else. Here there was a calm; no one was leaving; this was it—no point in making waves, moaning, or crying—so everyone was quiet. This was the first occasion I'd had to actually be in jail, to lie on a bed in a cell, stare at the ceiling, rue my wicked choices, and begin penance.

Just moments into the reflection though, I heard my first and last name called from the end of the cell-block. I jumped up and walked to the heavily bolted door at the end, where a warden was standing. "I'm Wendy Raebeck," I said.

"You're released."

With that, she unlocked the door and we took the long hike again. She led me to a dimly-lit locker-room and handed me a key to a locker. She then left me there, after pointing to a heavily secured door marked "EXIT," through which I was to depart.

Considering all the brouhaha, bells, and whistles I'd undergone to get IN this club, it seemed shockingly breezy to get OUT. (You'd think it would be easy to get in and hard to get out, but not so in my case.) Now nobody even cared that I was leaving, they didn't even watch me.

So I hopped out of my stripes and back into street clothes, grabbed my minimal effects from the locker, and pushed against the thick steel exit door.

Even more understated than the front or back entrances of this penitentiary, this little side door literally opened onto absolutely nothing. I stepped out to see the dark night all around—no porch, no driveway, no lights, just a vast lawn rolling down a hill. Too weird. I just stood outside the monstrous, painful brick building and wondered what the heck I was supposed to do now. (Thoughts probably similar to everyone else completing a prison sentence.) I had no clue where I was or how I'd get back to Venice Beach from here without a car.

Then, way down at the very bottom of the grassy hill, I spied two tiny figures clinging to the outside of a high chain-link fence topped with layers of coiled barbed wire. They spotted me at the same time and started jumping up and down, calling my name. It was Esmé and another neighbor who'd come to spring me.

And so I ambled down that hill, stupendously relieved, hungry but not `starving,' and duly fatigued by recent events. Esmé had managed to track me down in the system, and had somehow fished me back onto the radar. Who knows how long I might have otherwise been incarcerated?

About a month later, when my court case came up regarding that u-turn ticket, I told (an abridged version of) my story to the judge — so I wouldn't have to pony up that sixty bucks.

The judge listened intently to my tale. Then at the end, I asked, "Does my jail-time cover the cost of that ticket? The policemen said it would."

"Miss Raebeck," said the judge, "the experience that you've just recounted more than covers that ticket. You don't have to worry about it anymore." Then he gave his attention to the courtroom, "And to all of you listening, I hope this young lady's story has illustrated what some people are willing to go through to handle their responsibilities. And if you were thinking of giving me your whiny sob story today about why you can't pay your measly fine, I want you to seriously keep in mind what you just heard. This woman went to Sybil Brand County Jail to pay for a u-turn ticket. Let this be a lesson to all of you."

And Sybil Brand County Jail, actually built in 1963, suffered earthquake damage in 1994 and was consequently closed permanently in 1997. Since that time, it has been used as a regular location for movie and television filming. A highly convincing location, I can assure you—no set dressing required.

And, to those generous souls considering donating a maximum-security prison as your contribution to society, don't name it after yourself.

✳ ✳ ✳

TWO GUYS

I cut my departure times pretty close, can't even remember *strolling* to a departure gate. It just seems there's too much sitting already promised on flight day, might as well offset it with a sweaty sprint down the passageway and maybe an adrenalin burst at security check. Maybe all the scrambling adds excitement to the tedium of air travel, maybe my extra hour of sleep is worth the stress... whatever. I'm fully aware that other people get up earlier to catch a flight.

So, it was a normal day. I had an 8 a.m. flight from LA to NY. Terrorism was in fashion, as was charging passengers for luggage, so savvy travelers took these encumbrances into account. Only first-time flyers registered surprise at passenger lines half a block long or TSA not remotely caring that the missing passenger being paged right now is YOU. "Spread 'em" is the response when you whimper or sob, "I'm really gonna miss my plane."

It was a normal morning — I needed a 7:00 a.m. pick-up by the Super Shuttle and jaw-dropping luck at LAX. But, from the moment I'm picked up, my fate is out of my hands. I'm now officially on the conveyor belt that moves, or doesn't move, one and all one's cargo from Point A to Points B, C, D, and onward.

I greeted my shuttle driver with friendly urgency. "I'm really late, and the faster you go, the happier I'll be."

"I'll do the very best I can. What time's your flight?"

"8:00."

"You'll make it," he said, pulling swiftly into the traffic flow and grabbing the best lane.

In a perfect world, we could get there in sixteen minutes. Thrilled he was cooperative, I left him to his job, and asked how his morning was going.

"It's going great," he said. "Things are really, really great."

"Well, that's a good attitude. And it helps with everything, doesn't it?"

"Oh yeah. Works miracles, actually."

"Yeah, power of the mind," I nodded.

"I use it every day," he said, catching my eye in the rearview mirror.

"Oh yeah?"

"Yeah. Y'see, a few years back, I was in a head-on collision. It wasn't my fault—the other driver was drunk—but I almost died."

"What happened to you?" Now I was glad we had these few minutes.

"My legs were paralyzed and I was told I'd never walk again."

I scanned what I could see of the front seat for crutches, and wondered if he used a hand-device for the brake.

He continued, "That was what I got from the doctors. Second, third, and fourth opinions. No hope. I have an amazing wife, though, and she was right there, telling me she'd stay with me no matter what, that I didn't have to worry. But I told her I didn't accept it, I didn't believe it, and I'd be walking again as soon as I could."

This generic shuttle driver, an ordinary urban guy making an honest buck, elaborated about how he absolutely refused the doctors' decree. As months passed and he went from hospital bed to being able to sit, he held firmly to a vision of walking again. When he was finally given a wheelchair and taught how to use it, the first thing he did was try to move a leg or even a toe. But there was no sensation at all in his lower body.

As she'd said she would be, his wife was unwavering. He knew she didn't share his plan of a full healing. She seemed resigned to what the doctors told them. Still she remained loyally by his side while they adjusted to a completely different lifestyle. Understanding how much he yearned to walk again, she kept her uncertainty to herself. But he knew he was alone in his vision.

Despite everything, he never relinquished the certainty that he'd walk again. Each and every day he tried to somehow move his lower body. He didn't know how this was going to work, had no one to guide him, no one believing it would ever happen, but doggedly applied his will anyway.

Then one day, he moved one of his toes. Ever so slightly. He intentionally tried to move it and it moved. He knew in that moment that he was on his way.

From there, it was slow going...but, bit by bit, he increased his movement. Toes, then feet, then lifting a leg, then straightening out a leg. This took months and months. And still no one believed he'd ever walk. Finally he convinced the doctors to let him try standing.

And from there, ever so slowly, he began the process of...walking.

With ongoing tenacity and conviction, he was not only able to eventually ditch the wheelchair completely, but to actually run. The entire healing process took about two years, and his wife was by his side for every step.

"And now?" I asked, in awe.

"Everything's great," he smiled, "like I said when you asked me how my morning is going. I can walk, I can even run. Everything's great."

We were pulling up to my terminal now, at 7:15, and I just loved this guy for such brilliant motivation and for his strong and courageous story. As we said goodbye, I knew I'd brushed up against someone tapped into that human magic we all possess, yet rarely employ.

"And I know you'll catch your plane," he said.

If I lucked out inside, I probably would!

Ooh—but the lines were l-o-n-g. I lost an ill-afforded fifteen minutes on the check-in line, and still had more fuss ahead. From check-in, I was directed to a shocking security line that would cost me the flight if I had to wait it out. It was 7:35 now.

From my sad stance at the end of an endless line, I regarded the passengers in my vicinity to see if anybody else was freaking out.

Nope, they weren't tearing their hair out because they weren't late. They were good, left-brain planners, who probably had their full eight hours and a leisurely breakfast. "Over easy, honey, or sunny-side up?" They were probably taking 10:00 flights, or at least 9:00 ones. Not flights that had already finished boarding.

It was 7:40 now and I was practically pushing the person in front of me. Breathing down her collar. Clearing my throat audibly as if she should be doing something (like maybe pushing the person in front of her).

A couple of other passengers had now piled on behind me. "What time is your flight?" I turned to the guy behind me, out of sheer nervousness.

"8:00 to New York," he answered, surprisingly unconcerned.

"Oh! Me, too! How come you're not freaking out?"

"Cuz we're not gonna make it—there's no way."

"I gotta make it," I said firmly, dismissing his passivity. But it was all too clear we wouldn't do it from this outpost. "I'm gonna have to get to the front of this line somehow...."

"There's no way you can get through security and get to that plane in time," he said nonchalantly. "I'm just going through the motions in case the plane's delayed for some reason. Anyway, they'll put us on the next flight if we miss this one."

"Oh, when's the next flight?" Maybe there was hope.

"Tomorrow morning," he said, "same time."

"Oh, I can't wait till then!"

"Well, you're gonna have to, unless you want to pay for a new ticket."

But in my universe, as long as the plane was still on the ground, there was hope. "I'm gonna ask the people ahead of us if they'll let me through," I said. "In fact, if you stay close behind, I'll ask for both of us."

Frankly, I actually thought this down-head was pretty lucky I'd shown up. Now he could travel in my slipstream and make the flight. "We're not gonna make it," he repeated. "But try if you want."

I then pecked my way up the line, politely asking each person or group if "we" could cut ahead because "our" plane was about to leave. As hoped, they sensed my sincerity and kindly allowed "us" to crawl along to the front. It still took time, though—some people had to move luggage or kids out of the way, others didn't speak English. It was definitely a two-step. And as I begged my way along, I turned back to observe that my skeptical sidekick wasn't keeping up with me and was still a good ways back there. Though worming his way forward, he was possibly squandering a cosmic assist.

Meanwhile, I was now yanking off my shoes, positioning trays, and praying the avocado in my bag wouldn't be mistaken for a grenade—never know what bizarre interpretation a finnicky TSA worker might conjure up.

I was still hell-bent on making that flight, that is, if my hundred-yard dash was up to snuff. And while being frisked with the magnetic wand, I glanced back to see where my low-energy cohort had gotten to. But I couldn't spot him in the general mayhem.

"Thanks for the memories," I winked to the TSA woman who'd gotten to third base with me. Grabbing my carry-ons, avocado and all, I then saw that Mr. Negativity had drawn the unlucky number. Terrorist suspect of the hour, he was now seated in that unfortunate booth from whence no reason or departure time can rescue you. I couldn't catch his eye though and simply had to flee the scene.

At 7:50 I puffed up to the gate and leapt joyously to the tail-end of the stragglers' boarding line (my people). As we lumbered to the door, then down the jetway to the plane, I watched for my fellow late-nik. But he didn't come.

Once in my seat—grateful and sweaty—I continued to watch for the guy to board the plane last minute. And, as it happened, the flight was indeed delayed a few minutes. But soon it was all systems go, the door was shut, and we began backing away from the terminal.

He missed the plane.

As we taxied down the runway, I reflected on the two guys I'd shared the last hour with. First the brilliant optimist who'd chauffeured me to the terminal and then...the other side of the coin, equally as potent. Where the shuttle driver had used his will to overcome insane odds, with no guidance whatsoever, the man on the line—even when offered a surprise racehorse to hurdle all obstacles—somehow lacked even the wherewithal to grab the reins.

And my hectic morning chase to catch a plane had been accented by the power of choice, the power of our will (or lack of), and the pure magic of sheer determination.

✳ ✳ ✳

SHOWING UP

Every summer, Woody Allen would shoot a film in his native New York City. Production season there is during the warm months. In the late 1970's and early 1980's, this filmmaker was a lovable, local favorite. Original, funny, quirky, and driven, he not only continued to make everyone laugh, but produced, directed, and starred in box-office bonanzas. With his bespectacled geekiness and stated loathing of every place but New York, he was more like your downstairs neighbor than a leading man. But his neurotic self-deprecation was still good enough for the likes of Diane Keaton and Mia Farrow.

As a young actress, I was aware that Woody Allen had an eye for emerging actors. Numerous stars had their first memorable roles in his pictures. But to work with him would take some doing.

With acting, you've got to start at the beginning. Once I digested that and enrolled in scene-study classes, the rest began falling into place. In a surprisingly short time, I'd relocated to LA, gotten into the Screen Actors Guild, found an agent, and was making the rounds. With one film credit and one TV role, I was acclimatizing to the discomfort of the profession—where you're always waiting, and auditioning feels more like inarticulate begging. (Nowhere is it clearer that you desperately want what's being offered, thus you're rendered powerless.)

Hailing from NY, I'd go back there for the summer. For actors who didn't mind pounding hot pavement, there was work. Still new to the industry, I found `extra' work a way to get onto movie sets to learn about filmmaking. As a fresh young thing, I'd sometimes get upgraded to `day-player,' getting a line or two and higher pay. Not something to stay with, for me extra work was schooling. And maybe I could get onto a Woody Allen movie.

Like employers everywhere, casting offices needed dependable, professional actors who made their lives easier—actors who were eager to work, accepting of long and weird hours, and generally humble and flexible. Prima-donnas, wild cards, class clowns need not apply. But the nice thing about extra work was that it wasn't cut-throat; instead of one single part to compete for, there were tons of parts—street scenes, party scenes, store scenes. Movies are crawling with extras.

Relatively soon, I became someone the casting offices could rely on. I learned that it also paid off to pop into their offices periodically to pick up advance leads. And these impromptu visits sometimes resulted in a call-time for the next morning.

In 1978, Woody Allen was shooting "Manhattan" with Mariel Hemingway. I let my casting contacts know that I wished to be called if extras were needed for that. And, obligingly, they scheduled me for the first filming day. It would be a restaurant scene and we were told to "Dress as far out as possible. Don't be afraid to wear a helmet."

Probably every woman, especially those with fashionista mothers and grandmothers, has some little number in her closet that's too exotic or too something to ever see the light of day. In my boudoir was a powder-blue unitard under a flouncy, glittery, attached mini-skirt. Queen of the Roller Derby. This piece met the requirement.

Okay, okay, I know — I'm an extra, bottom of the barrel. Still, I arrive at the restaurant, crack of dawn, in my celestial get-up, confident I've followed wardrobe instructions and pleased to shake the dust off this sensational costume. And I'm quickly selected as the first extra to walk into the scene.

But things don't always go as hoped. Though I was there all day and befriended the Assistant Director (because after every take I ended up behind the camera, to remain there until the end of a long dialogue scene), and though I did get introduced to Woody (who constantly stepped behind the camera), that man was preoccupied. Like slightly. It's day one of a film he's producing, directing, and starring in; he's got a hundred people on the set — all on his payroll and waiting for their next command; plus it's his first working day with the lovely young Hemingway. Attila the Hun couldn't have taken him off task.

I went back to the casting office the following week and spoke to Adrian, the guy who'd tipped me off about squeaky-wheel-gets-the-grease. "Y'know," I said, "I was so dressed up for that scene in `Manhattan,' I think I could be in another part of the movie in regular street clothes and look like a different person. You think I could have another extra part in the movie?"

"Well," he said, "we really don't— It's frowned upon to have the same extras in more than one scene because somebody might notice."

"I realize that," I said, "but if you put me in some casual scene, I'd never be recognizable. I was hardly on camera in the first scene and probably wouldn't be in the second one either. Nobody's ever looking at extras anyway."

"Well, let's see how it goes," said Adrian.

And when I popped in two weeks later, he said, "Y'know, there's a scene coming up in Central Park. They need some people just walking by. We could probably put you in that pretty safely. Just wear jeans."

"Got it," I said.

So I'm in jeans and I'm `background action' in Central Park while one or two of the leads are walking by. In the shot, it begins to rain and everyone starts dashing. I'm one of the dashers. And just to make sure no one gets fired for casting me twice, I shield my face from the rain with a newspaper as I pass the camera.

Between takes, I go say hello to my buddy, the Assistant Director.

"Oh, hi," says he, "you're back. How're you doin'?"

"I'm good. I figured I could do another extra part since the first one was dressy and this one's casual."

"Oh cool, that's fine," he said. "Nobody's gonna notice in this scene."

But, as before, Woody was busy-busy-busy. And they shot our scene quickly, so I was cut loose.

And that's as far as it went that summer. But at least I got on the set and got to meet Woody Allen. Now I'd have to wait; hopefully he'd do another film next year.

The following summer, "Stardust Memories" was slated for production. Deeper into my career now, extra work was inappropriate, so I managed to get a meeting with Juliet Taylor, Woody Allen's casting director for principle parts.

"They're not shooting yet," she told me. "And I think Woody's already got his leads."

Still, it was nice meeting her.

One lovely weekend, I was at the wedding reception of some close friends. Another of the guests, someone I'd met before, now had a substantial production job on "Stardust Memories." This summer evening among intimate friends lent itself to more than small talk, and this super-nice guy, Daryl, ended up saying he'd see if he could do something for me vis-a-vis Woody's new movie. He definitely held no sway regarding casting, he said, but would see if he could effect anything. No promises, not a lot of optimism, but you never know.

Shortly thereafter, I received a call from a woman from the "Stardust Memories" office. She instructed me to come to the filming location in New Jersey on Sunday. A private bus for cast and crew would be leaving from 14th Street at 6 a.m. "Just be at the bus stop by 6, get on the bus, and come to the location," she said.

They had something for me; I didn't know or care what, and wasn't asking. Daryl obviously had orchestrated something. Because it was New York City and no one had cars, the means for getting everyone to a remote location was by charter bus. And, yes, an odd time and place to meet, but that's the business.

Excited, grateful, and somewhat nervous, I hated the idea of being tired for this important day, but that was a given—I'd be getting up well before 5.

I was staying down in Tribeca at the time, with my ex-lover, Zeke, still a friend, who'd also been at the wedding. Though aware of my Woody Allen designs, he maintained a blasé attitude about movies, TV, and Hollywood in general, viewing acting as `the vanity business.' But I was on a different page and, needless to say, was wired to see what I could accomplish in New Jersey. With no address out there, no phone number, I was to simply board the bus with everyone else scheduled that day, and show up on the set. I figured Daryl would be on hand to take it from there.

New York's a night place. Bars close at 4 a.m. Saturday night, the entire city goes out. And Sunday, they sleep in, then snuggle against pillows with the New York Times and coffee mugs, before going out to brunch after 12 noon. That being said, 6 a.m. Sunday morning doesn't even exist there. Six a.m. Sunday morning is like 3 a.m. anywhere else in the world—dead.

You learn this phenomenon when you need public transport at 5:15 Sunday morning.

I was way down near Chambers Street (a few blocks from Wall Street, obviously also a tomb), and intended to take a taxi. But in that location at that hour, there simply were none. Fortunately, the express subway could get me to 14th Street in fifteen minutes. That is, if a train were to come.

This morning, however, none did.

As I helplessly stood on the platform, listening hard for the train, minutes passed—five, ten, fifteen, twenty. I hadn't banked on a crazy delay like this.

I contemplated whether waiting for a cab might be a better bet at this point. But what if I raced back up to the street only to hear the train thundering by beneath me? It had to come soon.... I decided to wait it out, but wasn't feeling good.

A train eventually rolled in—not the `express' but the `local'—and things were looking grim. I now needed more than luck to catch that bus. My only hope was that the bus wouldn't leave punctually. Trouble was, I still had marathon racing ahead to get from the 14th Street subway stop to the assigned bus stop.

The train wasn't fast. And I felt my chance opportunity literally slipping away with the minutes and seconds. I didn't reach 14th till several minutes after 6, and still had to power down two long city blocks. I watched for the bus to maybe pass me so I could flag it down, but it didn't. It was 6:10 when I panted up to the designated corner, and there was no bus there. No nothing there, just the tombstone town as the sun came up.

Maybe I was in the wrong place, but I didn't think so. I just stood there, all dressed up with nowhere to go, feeling as dumb and self-sabotaged as a person ever could. I had no address in New Jersey, and no credit card to rent a car even if I did have an address. There was no one in the world to phone for any kind of assistance—it was 6 a.m. Sunday morning in New York City. I just stood there on the empty sidewalk. All I could do—without ever understanding the part of myself that would try so hard for something then royally blow it—was to accept the profound and inexplicable defeat.

As high and exhilarating as life can sometimes lift you, so can you, yourself, stick pins in the very balloon floating your basket.

You really have to be a roller-coaster lover to endure being an actor in film and television. At this time, I was living on strong coffee, street hotdogs, and diesel fumes from the city sidewalks. I wore my faithful white New York summer ensemble—a straight skirt and v-neck t-shirt, enhanced by strappy blue four-inch heels. With the city so filthy, the whiteness raised me above the grime. And at least I was tan and healthy from full days of chugging up and down Manhattan Island.

Then, one day in the middle of the summer, about six weeks after the tragedy, Juliet Taylor phoned and said, "You've got an interview with Woody Allen."

I was over the moon. An interview with Woody Allen. Just me and him.

The meeting was to be at a hotel on Central Park South—not glitzy, but old-school plush. I arrived at the appointed hour—crisp, fresh and four inches off the ground. This was going to be a laugh riot, we'd be slappin' our thighs and guffawing. I'd probably fall off my chair.

I was greeted at the door of the suite by an assistant of Juliet. As I entered, she introduced me to Woody, and offered a small armchair opposite where he was seated.

I had his full attention. He wasn't particularly animated, but certainly looked like that funny, self-effacing, totally unintimidating guy. He wasn't smiling, though. As I sat and he began the interview, he was actually deadpan, not jokey at all.

He didn't talk about "Stardust Memories," didn't talk about roles, just asked me questions and I responded. He gave me zero indication of his impression of me. Our meeting wasn't clinical, per se, but almost. He remained poker-faced the entire session, so sober it threw me. I mean, I knew this wasn't monkey business, but it wasn't a friggin' funeral. I don't think he even saw my pearly-whites.

I actually found it rather hard to be serious when the person you're chatting with is…Woody Allen. Please. Why be serious talking to Woody Allen? Even the thought of that is funny. Plus, I'm not particularly serious myself. And didn't want to start now. I should've said, "Who are we kidding here, Woody?" I should've.

But instead I went along with his little program. What a waste. I should've brought Mai Tais or something, should've asked if he liked my shoes. I don't know. He wasn't mean or off-putting, but he sure wasn't trying to win me over. Guess it boiled down to that miserable actor thing where it's so obvious you want something from the guy, something he probably can't supply, that it isn't a level playing field, and won't be a level playing field for one nano-second of the meeting.

Then, after what seemed more like applying for a paralegal position or possibly an embalmer job, I politely left.

I had been previously apprised that Woody in person wasn't like his movie character, that he could be quite intent and solemn. Trouble was, he looked like the funny guy, so I felt ambushed, like I'd gone to a tap-dancing audition only to find out it was ballet.

Maybe I didn't want to be in his stupid movies anyway, maybe he was as brooding and depressed as his characters indicated. I left, not deflated exactly—he'd been fully attentive—but I may have subconsciously realized that he wasn't looking for a nudge-nudge, wink-wink giggle-buddy, but support people he could play off. Straight men. He knew what he needed and it worked brilliantly for him. In all his pictures, one can observe that the lion's share of the humor comes from *his* character. (And, by the way, that's forty-seven films as of 2016, basically one per year for decades.)

Anyway, I never should've been a good dog at that interview. Probably should've dozed off after the first sixty seconds. Oh well, I gave it my best.

There was no follow up. I was not to be rewarded for my persistence. Summer continued and I kept abreast of "Stardust Memories," hearing that there were delays and things kept getting pushed back. But there was no conclusive word. I called Juliet Taylor once more.

"I haven't heard anything," she said. "As far as I know, things are on hold for the moment. But Woody does things his own way, I've learned not to bother him."

That summer, I was madly in love with an Englishman who lived in London. Madly in love. But we'd basically been apart since we met ten months earlier. Though all we wanted was to be together, we never could. We'd only seen each other a week here, ten days there, that kind of thing. Now I'd made my way from LA toward London, but had only gotten as far as New York. I had to work, for heaven's sakes. Then, finally, *finally* at the end of August, he was able to pool enough time and money to come to New York for a week.

We spent perhaps the most melodramatic, poverty-stricken, haphazard, humid, jinxed interlude in the history of romance. Then, in the middle of utter chaos, where we had nowhere to stay half the week, suddenly it was already time for him to return to London. Meanwhile, I had succumbed to getting a waitress job, starting mañana, at the Broome Street Bar in Soho.

This was in the days when everybody flew Freddy Laker to Europe to get low fares. But, to book a flight, you had to go line up the day before, then the first two hundred or so would get tickets. So lover-boy had to go out to Queens to stand on this line, and I accompanied him. Every second counted now, we were down to our final hours together.

As he stood on the line, I sat in a row of adjacent seats, my heart in my shoes. He was inching closer and closer to the wicked ticket counter; we were not going to be together anymore; I was going to be a waitress in the Broome Street Bar while he returned to London (for the fourth time since we met). I couldn't bear another cycle of missing him (all because of Woody Allen). After saying goodbye so many times, and truly suffering without him, it seemed impossible now to watch him leave again.

But there were only three people ahead of him. It was almost his turn.

I walked over to the line and held his hand. He looked down at me. "Buy two tickets," I said. "I'm going with you."

So he bought two. And the next day, I moved to London.

I told Zeke—the ex I'd been staying with earlier that summer—to please call me in London if anybody phoned regarding Woody Allen. "Call instantly and I'll jump on a red-eye and arrive next morning," I said. Thanks to Freddy Laker, this was possible and affordable. I had a New York answering service I'd also maintain and check daily from London. But I needed to leave a home phone number on file with Adrian and that casting office, so I gave Zeke's number, since it had also previously been mine. (This was decades before cell phones and email.)

Once in England, I reasoned I'd be okay since New York was only five hours away. If the movie called, I'd fly overnight and get there in the morning. Even if the call-time was for the next day, I could swing it.

So I moved in with my sweetheart. Madly in love, we were doing what lovers do when they finally get to be together. But every single day, Monday through Friday, I religiously checked my New York answering service. This ritual continued for about a month, with no word from Woody Allen. Then, one Friday, I decided to call Juliet Taylor's office directly. Summer was ending and I needed to know if the filming was over. But I didn't disclose my whereabouts to her.

"I still can't tell you much," said Juliet. "There could possibly still be a couple of smaller roles, but we wouldn't necessarily be told. At this point, we're basically just standing by to see if he needs us."

Having gotten the word from the horse's mouth that day, I didn't check my answering service. (Plus, all these calls cost plenty, and I was on Romeo's phone.)

That was Friday. Then Saturday went by, then Sunday.

Sunday night, Zeke called from New York. It probably wouldn't be false to say he felt jilted by me—though I chose to believe we had a lasting friendship. I had left him when

I relocated to LA, long before meeting my new English lover, but there's never much to be done about another's broken heart.

Sunday night, Zeke phoned and said, "Uh, the Woody Allen people have been lookin' for you."

"What?? What do you mean?"

"Well…they left a message here on Friday, and also on Saturday. They wanted you to— They, they were looking for you. I think they had a part for you."

"What? Why didn't you call me?" If anyone knew how important this was to me, it was Zeke.

"Well, y'know, I mean, different time zones, it's the weekend, I was busy…."

Now I was the one who was heartbroken. It was Sunday night. There was nothing I could do. Sunday night in New York….

I wondered if maybe they called my answering service, the one I didn't check on Friday. So I called there. Sure enough, there were messages from Adrian, "You're in the Woody Allen movie, and they're shooting tomorrow, Saturday. They asked for you by name. Call the office right now to get your instructions."

Oh God.

Even if I got a bit part or a day player, I now knew Woody Allen and could say hello. It could mean all kinds of things.

But now it was Sunday night in New York and everything was closed. I tried calling the casting office — of course it was closed.

I called back Monday morning, sorely ashamed that my ruse of pretending to be in New York had blatantly back-fired.

"Why didn't you get the messages?" Adrian wanted to know. "We left messages for you all over the place."

I had to come clean. He had been really good to me. "I'm actually in London," I admitted, "I'm really sorry—"

"What?!"

"This meant everything to me," I stammered, "and I have no excuse—I just didn't get the messages. It's totally my fault, I'm so sorry. Is there anything I can do?"

I didn't even have time to finish my outpouring because he started yelling at me. "Don't you EVER pretend you're in New York City when you're not! Don't you EVER leave the country and pretend that you're here! Don't you EVER not tell us when you're not in the country! If we have you as available, you are available. You have really let us down. There's no excuse. You know how things work, and what you've done reflects back on us."

And that was that.

It was now clear how hurt Zeke had been. Never underestimate the power of a wounded lover. There's probably some proverb about this. Or a hundred. And of course, for all of us, the musing is endless about careers versus love and relationships. All I knew was that, on that Freddy Laker line that day in New York, my lover was real and about to fly away again, and working with (the humorless) Woody Allen was only a pipe-dream.

As it happened, living in London was fruitful for my career. The film business there was far more refined and respectful than the Hollywood scramble. And, though I foiled my Woody Allen connection, I had my love, now uninterrupted by one more good-bye.

The only explanation I could ever manufacture for myself, regarding my dance around the unsuspecting Woody—who I truly believed might have cast me in a meaningful role at some point—was that, not only was it obviously not meant to be, not only was my subconscious shoving stardom off the map but, in terms of my overall life and everything that transpired thereafter, I feel there was a part of me (that I was always aware of as an actress) that shunned the notion of fame or fortune. In my deepest self, I dreaded the idea of being recognizable, known to the public, excessively wealthy, or having to live up to ultra-glamorous standards. And I don't think it's unusual to not crave the limelight; probably more normal, actually, to revere one's privacy and independence. I suspect only a rare breed is psychologically and spiritually equipped to deal with media, gossip, tabloids, expectations, invasion of privacy, ludicrous physical ideals, and mega-everything.

And, about two or three years later, I concluded that I didn't particularly enjoy being an actress—especially the beggar status that comes with the territory for all but superstars. (Though not literally begging for roles, it's disconcerting playing the game of life when everyone knows your hand.) As an actor-turned-rabbi friend of mine once said, "The best thing about being an actor is acting; the worst thing about being an actor is being an actor."

Amen to that.

But, probably even truer is what Woody Allen, himself, famously said, "Eighty percent of success is showing up."

❋ ❋ ❋

FAR OUT

———

Ever since an English medium named Sylvia connected me to my mother's spirit (coincidentally on the third anniversary of Mom's death), I've remained open to spirits and what they may have to impart.

After meeting Sylvia in 1972, and soon thereafter becoming inadvertently immersed in the waters, skies, rocky hills, and glorious everything of a Greek island, I found myself communing quite naturally with non-human surroundings. Not only was I receiving abundantly from trees and stones and goats and waves and stars and pomegranates, but I didn't miss my own genus. It was impossible not to acknowledge that this honesty, beauty, and simplicity I was taking in was more comfortable, more unencumbered, and more peaceful than I could ever receive from humans. This wasn't a conscious comparison, but more like an immense doorway to a vast world grander than I'd known or heard about.

And I learned to listen. I learned that the flow of natural law, natural beauty, and the changes of the wind, the light, and the seasons existed within me as well as without. I, too, am part of nature's liquid design. And with that awareness, sometimes came suggestions, in the form of words or sentences. Or answers might come from the sky, when I asked, or sometimes when I didn't ask. The information or direction was always straightforward, good, solid, and so obviously right.

This access, this comfort, this guidance, this safety net became…my god. He was like my own Greek god — an all-seeing presence who'd said hello on the Greek island, then never said goodbye.

Now it was fifteen years later, 1987, and I was living in Venice, California. With jubilation, I was on my first trip to Hawai'i, where I'd spend a whole month with a good friend who had moved to O'ahu.

Marie was busy freelancing, romancing, and getting established in her new Hawai'i home. On weekends, we'd beach and gad around together, and during the week, while she went to her gigs, I wrote newspaper articles for an LA paper in the Honolulu beach park.

The Hawaiian Islands, due to remoteness and endless ocean in all directions, are a world unto themselves. There's a lot going on.

My third week there, I headed off to Maui, where I also had friends. The first three days I spent with them, then set out in my rental car to see the rest of the island. I'd intentionally gotten a little hatchback, in which I could sleep at night. Balmy Hawaiian temperatures made this quite possible, especially for just a few days.

With little sense of direction, I took friends' advice and headed for Hana. The coastal road to Hana was exquisite and even afforded a distant view of a misty peak on another island off on the horizon. Not yet versed in Hawaiian topography, I didn't know it was Mauna Kea, the active volcano of the Big Island.

I stopped so often along the Hana Highway that darkness was falling when I reached Hana. But knowing the back of the car was my hotel, I wasn't overly concerned. It couldn't be too tough to find an undisturbed spot to park somewhere.

It would be odd to sleep alone in a car on a remote island in the middle of the Pacific Ocean, my whereabouts unknown to anyone. But I got comfy in the bedroll I fabricated beneath the `skylight' of the hatchback door. With the car windows partly open, the tropical breeze rustled in. And I lay silently breathing and appreciative under the starry, velvet sky.

It's not often you have the full night sky laid out before you as it was that night. Usually you're either standing up and it's tiring to keep craning upward, or you're with someone and a bit distracted, or you're shielded by the ceiling of a tent, or there's a cloud cover or city lights obscuring the wonder. Tonight the universe was all mine, sprawling to infinity, and I lay comfortably on my back, fully mesmerized.

As I pondered the firmament, lost in the constellations and loose thoughts they inspire, a darkish figure seemed to appear on one side of the sky. Of course it wasn't anything real, but there seemed to be a presence. A female…just a shadowy form amidst the astronomical display.

"Who are you?" I asked, as she seemed to linger and become more pronounced somehow.

"I'm a goddess."

I tried to see the form more clearly. I perceived long, dark, wavy Hawaiian-style hair flowing behind a woman's face in profile. She was maybe thirty-five or forty, a maturing woman, and I couldn't see her whole body, just down to about her waist. She appeared sort of like a figurine on the prow of a ship, protruding into the sky from one side. "What are you doing here?" I asked Her.

"I want to be in your life."

I wasn't open to this. "I already have a god," I told Her.

"I know," She said. "I'm not here to replace Him, I just think it's time for you to experience your female side more fully, and that's what I want to do for you."

"But I'm really content with my existing god," I said, feeling both nervous and foolish, but needing to defend my loyal deity.

The evening's entertainment was really throwing me. I thought I was all squared away, now here's this totally alien lady spirit crashing my life. I wasn't at all sure how to react to Her. All the while, I took Her at face value, was humbled to be chatting with Her, and fully intrigued by what She might signify or impart.

My original god then appeared (to my relief) in His formless way, on the other side of the sky, across from the goddess. Whew.

"What do you think about this?" I asked Him, as He took in the scene.

"I think you should accept Her," He said. Then reading my mind, continued, "I won't be leaving you — you'll have both of us. But She'll give you more of the feminine perspective. It's a good thing. You'll have both of us."

The goddess nodded.

I sighed. This was too much of a good thing.

But, hey, if my sacred spirit who'd hovered since Greek island days was giving Her the nod, how bad could it be? And I liked the novelty of it all, the possible new paradigm, and the yin-yang of balancing energies.

"Okay," I told Her, "if He's good with it, if He'll still be here, welcome aboard. I'm happy to meet you. And I look forward to whatever you offer. Just know…that it might take me a while to get used to you."

"Fine," She said. "I'll be available to you whenever you want. Try to remember I'm here. If you don't see me, you can always call on me."

And with that She faded. And then He did, too.

"Wow," I thought, feeling like a space traveler or as if I'd been dreaming. But I was wide awake, not even tired, and continued to ponder the stars, what had happened, and how real or unreal it was. You can totally ignore spirits if you choose, no one will ever know the difference. And since they're sort of invisible, you can always shrug off experiences with them. They're really imaginings to some extent, yet what they offer is so grand, why turn down the assistance? Why shut yourself off from an additional resource just because it's esoteric?

In my experience, esoteric had always been positive. I had no complaints about other dimensions, and never closed my shutters to guides and friends from other realms.

Back on O'ahu a few days later, I shared my goddess experience with Marie, wondering what she'd make of it.

"What did she look like?" Marie asked, surprisingly keen for the facts.

"She had real long, dark hair. She was Hawaiian, not real young but not old, and she was in profile—kind of like looking at a female wood-carving on the prow of ship. I could only see the top part of her, not her lower body at all."

"That was Pele," said Marie, "the Goddess of Fire."

"Who?"

"The Hawaiians call her Madame Pele," Marie said, "the Goddess of the Volcano, Mauna Kea, on the Big Island. She's the predominant deity in the Islands. Everybody knows Pele."

"Are you serious?!"

"Absolutely serious. She looks exactly as you described, and she's almost always depicted in profile. You met the Goddess of Fire. She's a really interesting goddess."

"I was right across the water from that volcano," I said. "I saw it before the sun set that night, but I didn't know until later what mountain it was or that it was the Big Island across the water from Hana."

There is much, much more about Madame Pele. Stories, folklore, legend, and mystery. She's renowned as a shape-shifter—one who appears in various forms and disappears just as lightly—and revered by all Hawaiians in that accepting way that local people recognize spirits uniquely their own. Greek gods, leprechauns, faeries, the Buddha, and so many others. There was no question in my mind it was She who'd appeared in the Hana night sky.

Later on, when I made Kaua'i my home for many years, I never spoke of meeting Pele. (Though the first dog friend I made shared Her name.) But, as the legend goes, Pele is known to intermittently reveal herself throughout the Islands. And on the rare occasions I heard tales from others who'd had encounters, I believed them, no matter how far out.

And legend also has it that Pele's bones remain on the island of Maui, creating a hill called Ka-Iwi-o-Pele (`the bones of Pele'). That hill is about two miles from where I met Her.

✳ ✳ ✳

TWINKLE, TWINKLE, LITTLE STAR

An only child, my mother grew up on Manhattan Island under the approving eye of her own mother, a German dressmaker, who outfitted not only the finer ladies of New York City but also her precious daughter. The fetching personality of the delightful Lotta (short for Charlotte) was only enhanced by her handmade pinafores and petticoats. Her ringlets, ribbons, and impeccable manners were all proof of her mother's constant attention and devotion. But, being German, Lotta could never be spoiled.

My grandmother, Gertrude, was hard-working and embraced The American Dream as most immigrants do. She'd learned to sew as a child, and found, through needle and thread, a way to set herself permanently free. Soon Gertrude could fabricate any design asked of her, and eventually made herself a remarkable career in New York City. Though she never saw herself as a stunner, she understood elegant refinery, and loved bestowing it upon others. So little Lotta was not only the recipient of Gertrude's adoration and style, but also a witness to the commitment and artistry of a self-made woman generations ahead of her time.

But despite being doted upon, Charlotte was a lonely child. Her regular evening pastime was to gaze out her apartment window to the building across Madison Avenue, where a young brood of six red-haired kids could be seen romping and frolicking every night. "They're always having so much fun," noted the somber Lotta in her clean, embroidered dresses. Those nights and that longing would later hold more sway over her destiny than anything Gertrude could wish for or engineer.

In high school, Charlotte shined. Her cleverness and buoyant goodness prevailed as she transformed into a thoroughbred. And in her graduating class of 1500 girls at Julia Richmond High School, she and one other student were voted Most Likely to Succeed. That other student was Betty Bacall.

The intended path for Charlotte was probably wealth and recognition, but such wasn't her experience growing up. Though poised for a life of leisure, when you considered Charlotte's entrepreneurial immigrant mother, her pragmatic German upbringing, and living through the Great Depression, (and soon World War II), Charlotte was unsure what she sought as she entered adulthood.

She pursued acting for a while, maybe as a passion, but surely also because stylish young beauties were frequently steered that way in New York City. But she also went to secretarial school to learn typing, shorthand, and workaday fundamentals that sensible girls acquired for paying jobs in a man's world. From there, she easily landed a receptionist job at National Biscuit Company.

At that time, she had also met a dapper young medical doctor who saw a future with her.

Enter Charlie, the down-to-earth guy who worked in the company mail room. With his avant-garde outlook, his cute disposition, whimsical words, and shy show of affection, he disarmed Charlotte completely. But the way he won a date with her was by offering to set her up with his much cooler (non-existent) older brother.

The courtship lasted years, as WWII commenced and Charlie joined the service. Charlotte knew she had to make up her mind. New York, doctor's wife, maybe an acting career? Or earthy, idealistic Charlie from Brooklyn—who also grew up with no siblings, who also envisioned a house full of kids.

One day, after Charlie got his wings, he gave Charlotte an ultimatum. "Tomorrow," he said, "I'll meet you on this same park bench, and you have to tell me if you're gonna be my wife. You've had plenty of time to think it over."

"Tomorrow?" asked Charlotte. "That's not very much time...."

"You've had four years to think it over," he said. If she didn't know by now, he was ready to let her go.

Somewhere deep down, Charlotte knew that with Charlie she'd be closing the door on Gertrude's agenda. He was a free-thinker who'd probably become a teacher or professor. It would be all about a big family, like the red-heads of her nightly childhood movie. With the doctor, it would be refined city life, upscale evenings, culture, hats, and gloves....

She married Charlie. They built their own home, by hand, in three acres of woods in North Carolina, and had six children. Chasing ideals, they moved often. But the parenting of kids, the camaraderie, dancing, singing, riding waves, and playing ball were a constant. As was dinner for eight every single night, as the family reconvened for spaghetti, meatloaf, or pork chops after a long school day. (Charlie was now a professor with a Ph.D.) Charlotte delighted in her little ones—who Gertrude tirelessly outfitted for years and years. Both Charlotte and Charlie cultivated the integral uniqueness of each child while making us tougher than they'd been. We weren't city kids or even New Yorkers.

It was good. We were doing what most of America was in the 1950's. Dogs and cats, bikes and baseballs. All summer off and a mother in the kitchen. We listened to Broadway musicals on record players and watched `The Mickey Mouse Club' and `Lassie' and `The Lone Ranger.'

This was what Charlotte bargained for, and her dream was alive when we were young. Later on, though, as we preferred our friends to our parents, as our lives became selfish and our home-life secondary, it was harder for Mom. This part of the program hadn't been outlined for her. We weren't faultless little kids anymore in darling clothes; we were autonomous, sometimes strident, outspoken teenagers announcing a new order. And there was no possible means of ever communicating to this new generation of Beatle-maniacs in mini-skirts why values and even God (God who?) mattered. What our parents had to say was irrelevant to us—a giant, empowered generation who had never done without, who couldn't grasp bread lines or war, who'd been blessed since birth by parents who gave us their all. For some reason I still don't understand, we had little respect for their generation, didn't want to be like them, and told them so. The world had somehow expanded, and we were out to prove it—to ourselves and generations to come.

Betty Bacall, meanwhile, had changed her name to Lauren, gone to Hollywood, become a star, and married Humphrey Bogart (just two months before Charlotte and Charlie got hitched). Mom quietly followed Bacall's career. And watching The Late Show and The Late Late Show— on which the actors of her era twinkled out to America— Mom was more at peace than when grappling with her kids' demands, quarrels, stubborn pouting, loud music, and all the trends that she sometimes found revolting.

Charlotte was partly shut out from the teenage reality dominating the house and partly disheartened. She drank more, entered her forties, and couldn't really envision herself growing old. Or even much older. With Hollywood's smoke and mirrors, Lauren Bacall, Judy Garland, Elizabeth Taylor, and the others somehow remained stunning. And the viewing public back then wasn't privy to the lighting, photography, and makeup magic that kept the audience glued to the screen. And the stars wore those sensational dresses Charlotte had no more occasion for.

Late at night, if I couldn't sleep, or went downstairs at 1:30 a.m. for some reason, there would be Mom, knitting, maybe smoking, maybe nursing the watery end of a mixed drink, and totally there with Johnny Carson or Jack Parr. This was her milieu, her true alter ego. And if Lauren Bacall happened to be on — though not someone Mom had been greatly drawn to in school, but who absolutely represented the opportunity not taken — Mom watched from across the years.

Was there just the slightest ache for the trail not traveled? I never thought Lauren Bacall was that beautiful or personable, and told Mom so when it seemed Bacall may have somehow won something Mom lost, though never spoke of.

And after Mom died, at only forty-five, I often thought back to those nights (every night, really, long after Charlie had gone to bed), and wondered, did The Late Show and The Late Late Show, and her hours alone with witty, city people of her own ilk make her happier than we did? Or is it just the pain of a reflective daughter wishing I'd been more mature?

Many years later, after Dad had remarried and everyone grew up, some even producing kids of their own, I had become a yoga instructor at Santa Monica Yoga. Another instructor named Leslie Bogart taught there also, and I soon learned that her father was Humphrey. And, sure enough, her mother was Lauren Bacall.

I found it not only coincidental, but somehow karmic that, some fifty years after graduating from Julia Richmond High School in New York, Mom and Lauren each had a daughter teaching yoga in the same studio three thousand miles away.

A couple of years went by, and my path rarely crossed Leslie Bogart's. When it did, it was at a teachers' meeting and not conducive to what I wanted to share with her. But one day, there was a potluck at another yoga teacher's home and we were both there. Mom had been gone over thirty years now, and I'd come to terms with most aspects of her life and death, yet I felt I owed it to her to connect with Leslie Bogart.

Toward the end of the party, I walked over to Leslie. "Hi," I said, "I wanted to talk to you briefly about something that has nothing to do with yoga or this party. Do you have a minute?"

"Sure," she said, her interest piqued.

"It goes back to New York City in the late 1930's," I said. "My mother graduated in the same high school class as your mother."

"Julia Richmond High School?"

"Yep."

"What was your mother's name?" Leslie asked.

"Charlotte Heider. Your mother would probably remember her. They weren't close friends, but the two of them were both voted Most Likely to Succeed."

"Sounds like my mother," said Leslie.

"My mother ended up dying young," I said, "at forty-five…."

"I'm sorry to hear that," said Leslie, sincerely.

"Yeah, it was hard…but it's okay now. Anyway, I just wanted to connect with you, kind of for her, because my mother was originally an actress, too, but because she was an only child and lonely growing up, she decided to get married and have a big family instead."

"My mother was an only child, too," said Leslie, "but she went the other way."

"Well," I continued, "my mother always followed your mother's career, and watched her success as the years went by. She'd see your mother in movies and on talk shows. And I think your mother symbolized to my mother the path she didn't take. And I found it ironic somehow that both their daughters would end up teaching yoga at the same studio out in California so many years later. And, in fact, my mother also named her first daughter Leslie."

"That is pretty odd," said Leslie, kind of moved. "Well," she looked me in the eye, "can I ask you something?"

"Sure."

"Was your mother a good mother?"

"She was a great mother," I said.

"Well, my mother sucked as a mother," said Leslie. "She was a terrible mother."

"Really?"

"Yes." And the hurt in her eyes was deep." And I wish your mother could've known that," she said. "She wouldn't have felt she didn't measure up. You're really, really lucky to have had a great mother." Leslie paused to let her message sink in. She wanted me (and my mother) to regret nothing. "And I'm truly sorry she died young," she said. "I would've given anything to have had a great mother." Now her eyes were wistful, as if the fortune of having a loving mother was something she'd always longed for.

And I knew, wherever Mom was beaming down from, that she heard what Leslie told me, and knew her choices hadn't been wrong ones, just different ones. She had followed her own stars, as I've followed mine. We can't have it all. Giant choices are part of every life. And we must give our all to what we choose. Love is what makes our choices right.

SOMEBODY HELP ME

After living the tropical-island fantasy for six years, I had to admit that a three-bedroom/two-bath house was baggy on me. I loved it and would keep it, but perhaps someone else should foot the bill for a while.

I rented out the house to a couple. She was a substitute teacher, he a chatty art teacher. And there were two young grown sons, one who worked at Costco and the other remained a mystery—I was never to meet him.

I started the Hernandez gang with a six-month lease. I'd learned, through owning an additional rental property, to keep leases short until tenants proved themselves. So, with my lovely home in their seemingly stable hands, I prepared to spend time on the Mainland with my eighty-eight-year-old pop. Though way out on Eastern Long Island, I'd still be just a phone call away from the Islands. And my trusted handyman, Homer, agreed to jump in for any emergencies.

As an absentee landlady, things didn't go too badly. And it was awesome renting an apartment next door to Dad and spending time with the white-haired one. At that tender age, nothing is taken for granted.

Then one day on the phone, Homer mentioned having run into Carlos Hernandez, someone who made candid dissertations about his opinions and lifestyle until someone stuffed a bandana or banana into his pie-hole. I'd observed the tendency upon meeting him, but figured it was his wife's and his sons' problem, not mine. Now Homer was parlaying what the talkative tenant had shared in the parking lot behind Brick Oven Pizza. Apparently, Carlos had been in a rush to get home because he had a sexy date with his wife that night. A romantic evening for these two, Carlos had confided, was to take psychotropic drugs, go to bed, and stay there all weekend. (This couple was pushing fifty.)

Landlords love hearing this stuff.

"Yeah," Carlos had continued, "we're both into the same thing. It's a great relationship."

It had also recently been leaked that their jobs had sort of dissolved (or been retracted, if in fact they ever had said jobs), and their sons were covering the rent. Not what you want to hear when you're watching Lawrence Welk re-runs with your father and step-mother six thousand miles away.

The next event, that didn't altogether throw me after the Brick Oven snippet, was when November first arrived and the rent did not.

When I telephoned Carlos about it, he played footsie for a few days while I politely spelled out the lawful protocol I'd be obliged to follow should the rent remain unpaid. They only had two weeks left on the lease, and I was due back to the island on their last day, so the situation wasn't dire. But I'd only collected half a month's deposit from them (foolish leniency in my haste to get to the Mainland).

But the red flag whizzes up the flagpole when tenants don't pay rent. The legal route is stressful, can be costly, and doesn't guarantee any recouping of losses. But Carlos and Kimberly, who left their charm in the classroom, did not pay, and declared that they were staying in the house after the lease ended (next week), because they had nowhere to go. Was I going to put them on the street? they asked accusingly. Had I no sympathy (for parents who live off their son's Costco wages)?

After advising them that I was forced to adhere to the terms of the lease, I conversed no further, leaving them to wonder what I'd do next. Meanwhile, I was left to my own homespun solutions, since my frail father said this predicament was beyond his scope as he'd never been a landlord. Our roles had begun to reverse anyway, and I couldn't drag him into it. But what the heck would I do if the Hernandez' refused to leave?

I had white-lied to them that I, myself, was moving back into the house the day after their lease ended, but I had no idea how much gall they had. Did they really have nowhere to go? There are certainly droves of unseemly renters who know precisely which laws will bend in their favor.

This is when being a single woman doesn't mesh with landlording. Me on their porch bearing a white envelope wouldn't be much scarier than Peter Cottontail thumping his foot against the front door—it wasn't going to work. And Homer the Handyman—bless him for being there for me in a hundred ways these last six years—couldn't be enlisted now because he was over seventy, small and skinny, and had the mushy trait of wanting everyone to like him. In the tough-guy role, he'd be even worse than me or the rabbit.

What was I to do?

So I phoned the son at Costco. He was comfortingly sympathetic, agreed his parents' behavior was shabby, but said he was sick of them, too, and was moving to his own place now that the lease was up. He said his folks had given him the same out-on-the-street sob story, and not for the first time in his adult life. (Carlos and Kimberly, I now knew why, had insisted both their sons' names be on the lease with theirs).

What was I going to do?

A real estate attorney I phoned only floored me with the costs I'd accrue should I hire him. He recommended I follow every possible legal procedure on my own first and only call him back as a last resort. So I had Homer deliver the standard `Five-day or Quit' notice, and nothing transpired after that.

Of course I imagined a protracted stand-off for weeks or even months, as I paid the mortgage and the weekend warriors tripped out in my brand new queen bed. "I need back-up," I thought. "If they don't move out, I have to show up with someone more substantial than Homer or Mr. Cottontail. I need credibility." It wasn't about intimidation, but just to show that this lone little landlady wasn't dangling from the lease like a kite-tail in the wind. Oh, for some brothers…but mine lived on Long Island and wouldn't be spending a grand to play a five-minute cameo on some Hawaiian porch.

I tried to think of who I knew on the island who was big and tall and strong and might be willing to stand beside me at the door as I fanned myself with the white envelope. Two male friends came to mind, but like Homer, they were under-qualified for the assignment. I needed someone BIG. Someone to do that guy thing I'd seen in the movies, where the brute shows up and everyone quakes in surrender. But I couldn't think of anyone appropriate.

Then suddenly I thought of Porter, a neighbor a few blocks over. He was a local man of about 6' 2" with a shiny macho truck matching a shiny, macho physique. A grazing bull, too strong for comfort. Porter! I knew him fairly well. He'd been a massage client and we'd had neighborly chats over the years. Making him even more of a candidate, he seemed to really be something of a tough guy. From a long-standing line of ranchers, he had lots of land, cattle, and horses, and was possibly even familiar with the shady politics of local government.

But I didn't have his phone number. And though I'd oft seen him driving down my street or around town, I didn't even know where his house was.

Okay, who else? Think, think, think. A guy named Will then sprang to mind. Will would be perfect for this! I only knew him superficially, but he measured about 6'5", had a construction business, and could regularly be spotted jogging along back country lanes. He had a truck and a Hummer, and a chest-span that made both men and women weak in the knees. His posture, ponytail, and piercing baby blues made you truly believe in kale.

But I didn't have his number either, nor knew where he lived.

At least I was getting somewhere…if I could just find these two—both the kind of guys Bruce Willis would kill to look like. Nobody—not Carlos, not Kimberly, not nobody—could look these characters in the face and say, "We're not budging." It was laughable. And I was mollified to have lit on a plan.

So, the Hernandez lease expired the same day I got back to the island. I wasn't truly planning to move back into the house as I'd fibbed to Carlos and Kimberly. I was moving into the recently-vacated back unit of my rental property instead.

But upon landing, I did a quick drive-by of the house under siege. Predictably, the Hernandez car was there, the house still occupied, and no signs of exodus.

I went back to my rental property, slept off the trip, and woke up ready to do whatever I could to retrieve my property from the creative couple. But first I had a massage job scheduled, so I scurried off to perform it at a nearby resort.

In my haste, however, I forgot my coconut oil. So, with apologies to the client, I trotted out to an adjacent market to score some. Approaching the store, I heard someone behind me call out my name. I turned to see Porter full of morning aloha.

"Porter! I can't believe I'm running into you! I just got back last night, but I need to talk to you about something. I'm hoping maybe you can do me an odd favor."

He eyed me with curiosity, as I gave him a severely abridged run-down of my stalemate, ending with my brilliant solution that featured him and/or Will. I knew he'd agree to help and now the whole miserable ordeal would be behind me in a matter of hours. What serendipity — here he was!

"I can't do that," said Porter, not even thinking it over.

"Why not? It will only take a few minutes."

"It's not right," he said.

"I know," I stammered, "but I don't know what else to do, and I really think this will work."

"It won't work," said Porter, again not even thinking it over. "That kind of thing never works. Because it's not right."

What could I say to that?

"You don't want to intimidate them," he went on. "That's not the way to handle it."

"I know it's not, but I can't think of anything else to do. I'm over a barrel. I've already served them papers, but they say they're not leaving. If it's just me trying to get them out, they're not going to leave."

"It's not just you," Porter said, "you have to have higher faith. You always have to do the right thing, even if you're not sure of the outcome. You can't sink to their level. It never works anyway." He was pretty sure about all this.

"I know you're right," I admitted. "I just feel a bit desperate."

"You'll be okay," he said paternally. "It will work out. You'll figure out how to handle it." Again, Porter seemed surprisingly confident despite leaving me no strategy at all.

I had to race back to my massage client, so I sincerely thanked him and gave him a hug. He'd shown me a side of himself I hadn't known about. Here was this big macho hulk steering me back to the high road.

I completed my massage, then zipped to a nearby grocery store to grab some sustenance. Again, a voice behind me called out my name. This time I turned to face the mighty Will.

Now I couldn't contain my surprise. "This is amazing," I told him. "There were two specific people on this entire island that I needed to talk to—both of whom I had no idea how I was going to find—and the first two people I run into after just getting back late last night are the exact two I was looking for."

"What's up?" asked Will, wondering why I'd be seeking him—first time in six years. I, meanwhile, was pretending he was Mr. Wrong, in order to stay on topic. (Porter was married, but Will was some celibate born-again something or other.)

I disclosed my Hernandez story, topped with my stand-on-the-porch plot—albeit slightly deflated, thanks to Porter's spiritual nudge. But I didn't divulge Porter's refusal; I still had wind in my sails. And Will had clearly been delivered to me for this exact purpose. There was no other possible explanation for him getting coffee at the precise moment I needed him to. I'd never even seen him in that store before.

"You can't do that," said Will.

"I can't?" I was taken aback. Again. Another Olympian balking at this cream-puff task?

"No," he shook his head, "it's not right. You have to go about it differently."

That I was a lone traveler on the low road was being driven home pretty hard now. And I had thought my plan was so clever, so rough and tumble.

"What do you mean?" I asked. "I just feel like I can't approach them all by myself. I don't think it will work."

"You don't do it all by yourself. You don't ever do anything all by yourself. You have to ask God to help you."

"Well, that's an idea," I agreed. (Truthfully, I'd been so busy worrying I hadn't really offered it up to the Greater Good.)

"Would you be comfortable if we prayed about it together?" Will asked.

"Uh, yeah...." though I wasn't sure what he had in mind. "Where?"

"Right here."

"In Foodland??"

"Yeah," he parked his coffee on the doughnut counter. "We'll just step over here...." and he walked ten steps into the Hawaiian souvenir section.

Then, beside the flowered sarongs and shot glasses emblazoned with maps of our island, Will took both my hands, closed his eyes, and began a lucid and detailed prayer, punctuated a bit too frequently with `Father' and `Our Lord.' He succinctly outlined to the Almighty, in no uncertain terms, what we needed done: these tenants had to pack up and go, with no further ado.

I'd never really heard anyone instructing the higher powers with such authority and precision. I thought we earthlings were supposed to be the servants, but my spiritual prowess obviously needed an overhaul. But Will was as serious about this as he was about everything else, and covered the bases so thoroughly there was no way God could get the instructions wrong.

"Can I add something?" I asked quickly, before the `amen' cut us off from the heavenly hot-line.

"Sure," said Will, visibly surprised since he thought he'd said it all.

"Dear God," I began, "I just want to thank you for sending me Porter and Will this morning, who've both really helped me see that You are the one who can help me. And please forgive me for thinking that a scheme would be a solution to my problem. I will trust You to help me instead."

"Amen," Will and I said together.

Then we hugged and smiled, and I thanked him most sincerely.

As I drank my hot chocolate and reviewed my morning—and even now, as I write this years later—it's clear who placed Porter and Will, two forces of nature, in my path that day. And even why they were the ones who came to mind when I needed help, even though I'd wished to consign them differently than the way in which they actually served.

On my way home, where I had unpacking to do and worries to attend to, I took another casual drive past the house to see what the Hernandez' might be up to.

As I drove by, I saw their station wagon backed in close to the house. The tailgate was down, and boxes could be seen nearby. They were moving out.

PROXY MOXIE

"How's Mom?" was the first thing I asked once Dad and I got out of the JFK maze. She'd been in bed my whole freshman year of college, riding out the cancer nightmare that, back then, was even more hellish since alternatives were non-existent.

Despite remaining bedridden, Mom's frequent and upbeat letters continually declared she was "really on the road to recovery now." I believed her. Mothers don't lie. Now I'd get Dad's take on it. I watched him driving, his hard gaze locked on the expressway.

"Those doctors are all bastards," he said, with uncharacteristic venom. I took a half-breath and waited. "They all lie," he said, the words themselves painful to utter.

"What are they lying about?"

He glanced over at me, maybe to decide if I was old enough, strong enough.

"They keep telling me she's getting better, but she isn't. They're all liars."

"She isn't getting better?"

"I give her two months," Dad said. The worst sentence I had ever heard.

"Two months? Two months to…?"

"Two months to live."

His words froze in the air and stayed there. Fifty years later, they're still there.

So I guessed that Mom had been lying, too, but I could hope Dad was wrong.

Dad had an uncanny grasp on the life force, though. He somehow knew its tune, knew the dance, when to twirl, when to slow dance, when to sit down and rest. He read life's subtleties and knew when to get quiet and not bargain with demons.

He told me, decades later, that in Mom's case, he had suggested a holistic path to her (though that term didn't yet exist), but Mom had held up one hand in a firm no. Maybe she trusted her doctors, maybe her spiritual sands were running out for reasons we couldn't ascertain. But we were never to find out—six weeks after Dad's words on the expressway, she was gone.

With his heart, and all our hearts, in a million pieces, my father then took on natural health with a vengeance—even though it was an absolutely alien concept back in 1969. That Mom hadn't taken care of herself was as factual as the Tang, Bisquick, and Aunt Jemima in our kitchen cupboards—that Dad summarily trashed in a big sweep just days into our new life.

From that moment, he rigorously sought out any and all reading on true wellness and how it's achieved. Consuming every book he could discover, his grief fueled his education. As a professor, sharing what inspired him was second nature, and I, his wounded disciple, was starved for anything I could get from this last parent. We were both grateful for a fellow student in our new study, he voraciously devouring resource material then acting out the advice in garden and kitchen while I trotted along behind, snapping up each book the minute he turned the last page.

Mom's death hovered as our reason to live better. Inadvertently, she'd taught us to keep the reins of our own lives, to heed warnings, and trust the laws of health—one of the simplest truths being, "The natural state of the body is one of healing—if we allow the body to do so." Fasting and consuming raw, fibrous fruits and vegetables completed the basic instruction Dad and I learned to lean on.

This knowledge and practice, though spotty much of the time and ever tarnished by temptation, bonded my father and me. After he turned me onto the good Doctor Shelton in Texas, I'd gone out there in 1974 and fasted on water. Then, a few years later, Dad and his second wife, Darlene, made the pilgrimage, too, and fasted thirty days each. Thereafter, Dad always regarded those weeks in San Antonio as a turning point in his health. After cleansing to the bone marrow, he remained forever thankful for that new lease on life. In his late eighties, he credited that fast as key to his longevity.

He enjoyed his whiskey, though. And, once down the hatch, the raw veggie crudité he and Darlene noshed at sunset was mildly marinated in Jack Daniels. And, by eighty-seven or eighty-eight, Popsy had had an episode or two—mini-strokes, he called them, close calls, sometimes causing garbled speech. He even learned to identify a "pre-stroke headache," a painful warning to lie low and not mess around. On these scary occasions, he'd stay in his pj's a day or two and reluctantly succumb to Advil.

It was at this time I slayed all logic and chose to move from Hawai'i to his remote North Fork village on Long

Island. I'd promised myself years earlier to spend time with him when he grew old. With these strokes, I dared not wait longer. And I knew, regardless of outcome, living near an elderly parent—something you can either do or not do— wouldn't be regretted, despite the challenges to pull it off.

With that niggling cocktail habit, Dad could be unpredictable, though, causing me to occasionally kick myself for relocating from Paradise. He, meanwhile, grew less and less mobile, yet maintained that keen mind and precious silly streak as indicators that he wasn't winding down. (And Capricorns are `cursed with longevity.')

Eventually, though, I had to return to Hawai'i for a spell to catch up on my responsibilities.

But three months after my return to the Islands, Dad had another incident. Though he might have preferred to ride it out, his care fell to Darlene, who called an ambulance. Next thing we all knew, Dad (almost ninety now) was in Stony Brook University Hospital two hours from his retirement community, heavily medicated, and being assessed for this, that, and God knew what. And all the oversight fell to his wife, who became his health proxy. Questioning authority, though, was Dad's forte, not hers, and he was sedated to the eyeballs.

Soon days and days were passing with no progress nor even progress report. Just fruitless chatter with no directives to get him home. The final word, apparently, had to come from Darlene, who seemed oddly `frozen' (as Dad had tagged an emerging tendency of hers). And, according to a couple of on-site siblings, Dad couldn't possibly pull through under such heavy meds. Things looked bleak. The hospital, admittedly, had no clue what actually had happened to him, what his official status was, and what to do next. Essentially, no one was at the helm while Dad, allegedly, was `speaking in tongues.'

Still in Hawai'i, I somehow managed to get a phone to his ear in the hospital. What I gleaned from his garbled speech and uncanny good humor was that he was totally immobilized probably due to drugs, frantically wanted out, and feared for his life. "But you can't tell anyone here what you really think or feel," he confided, "or they'll let loose the lepers of the land." This was the kind of talk labeling him `not in his right mind,' when in fact he was clearer than anyone, just severely challenged.

"Dad," I asked, "what do you think would be the best way to get you out of there?"

"Bring the mob," he said.

I had to giggle. "I'm not sure how much of a mob there is right now, but I'll see what I can do."

"Bring the mob," he repeated. (You can take the man out of Brooklyn, but you can't take Brooklyn out of the man.)

It was definitely going to take muscle to make something happen in that joint, situated hours from where family members lived. Plus, everyone had to work every day, so siblings were dropping in on their own schedules and unable to communally strategize. And I, due to the five-hour time differential, was regarded as `absentee' by the clan.

Registering the general chaos, I phoned an appropriate hospital staffer to root out what the hold-up was. I was told Dad couldn't be released until it was verified there were both a bed and medical personnel ready to receive him somewhere. So the hospital was waiting for Darlene to provide that information, but there was no movement.

I then phoned the relevant entity at Dad's retirement community, who agreed to fax the hospital that, yes, the skilled nursing facility (called The Shores) was ready to receive and care for him since he was too weak to return to his house.

But after having been in that hospital fifteen days, Dad was lagging. His system couldn't take much more of lying there drugged and motionless, with no hope of escape. According to siblings, he could no longer move any part of his body. And they were immeasurably concerned.

So I jumped on a plane, went directly to the hospital from JFK, and found the tortured patient. Super weak, he couldn't move at all or even turn his head side to side, but was relieved to see me. "We're gettin' you outta here, Dad," I assured him, then sat by his bed until almost midnight. Underneath all the confusion, absence of intel, discomfort, extreme weakness, lack of leadership, and horrible food, I could see his lights were still on, though dim.

I got back to my trusty boarding house late that night, grabbed a few winks, and drove back to the hospital at dawn. All morning I worked the connections I'd made by phone and, by the end of the day, the paperwork had been faxed, an ambulance would be sent for Dad the next morning, the hospital would free him, and Darlene had signed the documents.

Whew.

But just when we finally freed Dad, hoping he'd pull through and resume his life, things got complicated. At The Shores, the skilled nursing facility of his retirement community that housed a dwindling population of medicated, semi-present, chair-bound elders, Dad was received as not just an invalid but a newbie. None of the staff knew his holistic leanings. They didn't speak that language, nor were they permitted to deviate even slightly from medical protocol.

It was with additional distress we all now observed numerous, advanced bedsores all over Dad's arms, legs, feet, and lower back from those sixteen stationary days at Stony Brook Hospital. That a high-profile, academically-acclaimed university hospital wouldn't rotate a patient who's bedridden for that duration was beyond shocking.

Adding to the difficulty, my request for a list of Dad's medications (he was now on fourteen different ones) wasn't smiled upon. And in no time, I was enlightened that Darlene was his health proxy, she alone would be given information, she alone could discuss things with nurses and doctors, she alone could make suggestions and decisions.

Dad, meanwhile, was in diapers and could no longer walk; his leg muscles had atrophied completely during the past two weeks. Plus, he remained drugged up the wazoo. While adjusting to a severely limited future in the skilled nursing facility (a place he'd always dreaded), and covered in bedsores, he somehow played the cordial host to anyone who dropped in—Darlene and myself every day, due to our proximity, and a rotation of his other offspring, all ill at ease to witness our patriarch in such a pickle.

Living right next door, I was able to sit by Dad's bedside late at night discussing what he wanted, what his options might be, and what approaches might fly in this counterintuitive holding tank. We'd make solid plans about limiting his medications, securing his costly and hard-to-procure holistic supplements from Darlene's kitchen table (nixed by medical overseers so as not to interfere with their toxic tablets), and practicing what he needed to say and to whom. But the next day, our plan would invariably dissolve. Dad would cave to nurses or Darlene, even nudging me under the bus if I chimed in on behalf of the holistic practices he constantly told me he longed for.

Poor Dad, I had to forgive him because he was eighty-nine, so vulnerable, and under influences. My three sisters at least were in my camp, if only by phone. But his beloved natural supplements, that he had come to swear by in recent years, remained on the kitchen table.

Meanwhile, I was getting subliminal messages that would eventually take root in my soul. One was that the transitions that the very old face can be beyond our imaginings, beyond our coping mechanisms, and beyond our control. Bizarre situations advance with their own energy, regardless of well-intentioned bystanders. And there are factors at work that don't meet the eye, such as relationship loyalties, spiritual safety nets, and even a patient's own silent game-plan for getting what he or she needs. What may appear all wrong might just play out better than onlookers expect.

After two weeks of doing all I could, I had to get back to Hawai'i again. I'd made little headway in helping Dad, and had caused ripples, too, by inquiring about freaky procedures that other relations consented to. Doctors were not to be questioned? And when I cited Dad's holistic history, suddenly no one shared the memories. `Natural health' was now a dirty word.

Fortunately, the owners of my rooming house allowed me to leave my car and possessions there, knowing I'd be back. So I returned to Hawai'i with a heavy heart and a light purse.

For reasons Dad's kids were not to comprehend, he never got a telephone in his room. Thus, my only updates about his condition would be via Darlene, someone who, in fifty years, had phoned me maybe three times. But when I called skilled nursing directly, I was bluntly reminded that only his health proxy could inquire about his condition. I'd made my way onto the trouble-maker list—evil-doers who suggest juice instead of Sprite, who adjust room thermometers if it's horribly stuffy or freezing, who massage a patient's feet and legs, or ask the 10 p.m. nurse to please douse the fluorescents before leaving Dad for the night. Trouble-maker!

However…Dad was one month shy of ninety. He'd had a great run. If this was it, it was hardly a bum deal. And I'd spent most of the last year living next door. Yet, perplexingly, my father remained in good spirits despite what might otherwise be perceived as a horror show.

It was mid-December, 2011. I'd been back in Hawai'i again two weeks, tending my rescued kitten, working hard to make up for lost income, and preparing my first book for publication.

But things weren't going well for Daddy-o. His bedsores worsened (from being improperly treated), and he then contracted MRSA, a contagious infection medical workers are terrified of. Forced to call Darlene, I learned that Dad was going into the local hospital for surgery; the MRSA in the bedsore on his lower back had to be cleaned out.

Seriously? They were going to cut his low back open? All because of Stony Brook Hospital's neglect and skilled nursing's mistreatment of a bedsore? As a bodyworker, it seemed obvious that bedsores need the opposite of the stagnation that caused them; they need to be aerated and gently soothed; they need light, blood-flow, and a body that is moving. But the medical treatment was to smear thick ointment on the sores, bury them under plastic bandages, then leave Dad in that identical, festering, supine position that created the mess in the first place.

Hearing about the impending surgery, I phoned Dad's doctor (a total apparition), to find out what info Darlene was getting. Doctor Scheinbaum was like one of those cops who's going to give you that ticket no matter what. On the phone, he couldn't conceal his tedium with this distant, nosey relation whose queries only underscored her medical ignorance. "Your father has two months to live," he said matter-of-factly.

"You don't know that."

"Three at the most." And he continued in an insulting monotone, as if talking about a train schedule.

"Doctor Scheinbaum, you're talking right over me."

Scheinbaum took a quick breath, wanting even more to terminate this call. "There's nothing else I can tell you. We're going to perform the surgery to get rid of the infection, but the chances of healing are very low, due to his age and his condition."

"Those doctors are all liars," I could hear Dad saying about Mom, now forty-two years ago.

"I'll let you go," I said. It was all so ironic and unfair that Dad, of all people, should end up helplessly cornered by the medical system, without anyone backing him. Neither he nor I ever fathomed things could turn out this way.

My sister Lola and I then discussed at length where we could possibly take him if we could somehow rescue him. His life was undeniably at stake, his chances decreasing daily. No one was considering his desires or point of view, and he was the one with the comprehensive grasp on healing. Lola and I agreed on the kind of loving care he needed, but neither of us could provide it; she was staying with her young son, and I lived in Hawai'i. And no one else was on our wavelength. A lot of painful truths about old people and what happens to them were coming home to roost. Some of us, including Dad, just never thought this would happen in our family.

The day after Scheinbaum shined me on, I received an email from my brother: "This is just to let everybody know that it's been decided to put Dad into hospice. Due to his tough circumstances, everyone agrees this is for the best and it is time."

H-O-S-P-I-C-E?

`Morphine and ice cream' had always been my nickname for hospice. (When the patient's will is being overridden.)

Let me clarify here: though not a wealthy man, Dad's retirement plan could fully accommodate as many years as he and Darlene could last, and they intended to do so "in grace and dignity," to quote Dad himself. His new digs in skilled nursing cost the family nothing, all was covered in his original arrangement with the retirement community. The reasoning behind this hospice declaration, therefore, seemed out in left field.

In studying the hospice email, I noticed that it hadn't been sent to my three sisters, only to the families of my two brothers and two step-brothers. So I quickly phoned the brother who sent it.

Surprised to hear from me, he said, "You weren't supposed to get that email."

"Why not?"

"It was just a decision that was made by those of us that live nearby. Everyone thinks it's the best thing."

All but speechless, I managed to say, "You all decided to put Dad in hospice without talking to me or any of our sisters?"

"Darlene met with the hospice people and everyone thinks it's the right time. It was her decision, but she consulted with us and people all feel it's for the best."

"*Hospice?* Do you understand what hospice is?"

"Of course I do."

"Well, I'm ashamed of all of you."

Breathlessly, I then phoned Lola, my only sibling who felt the eeriness of Dad being stripped of any say in his own treatment. "Did you get the email?" I asked her.

"What email?"

"The one about Dad going to hospice."

"Dad's going to hospice?"

"No, he's NOT! But the family's trying to put him in."

"Who? Who in the family? No one talked to me."

"It's just the boys and Darlene—they've all decided, without any discussion with the rest of us."

"What? When?"

"I don't know. Soon."

"We gotta get him out," we said simultaneously.

"If I can get a flight, can you meet me at the airport tomorrow?"

Lola was a born first-responder, precisely who you wanted by your side when push came to shove. "Definitely," she said. "But why would they DO that?"

"God knows. Anyway, let me see if I can get a flight. But don't tell anyone in the family that I'm coming—we'll have to work this out on our own."

With fancy footwork and legitimate urgency—life or death—I got a plane that night. Lola agreed to meet me at LaGuardia the next afternoon. And, thankfully, I had that rented room and car available at the other end. As for little White Boy, the unsuspecting kitten, he'd have to ride along because who knew when I'd be back?

We scrambled to catch the plane, then flew the ten hours overnight to New York. Lola and her daughter, Chancy, grabbed us at the curb in their pickup, then we four headed to the end of Long Island's North Fork where we knew poor Dad was recovering from the surgery.

Pondering everything about our imminent challenge, we zoomed the two and a half hours to Dad's hospital, that was situated in a picturesque marina equipped with even a boat ramp, should patients arrive by sea. (Boating and drinking were both favorite local sports that kept the hospital on its toes.)

Arriving at 7 p.m.—White Boy hanging tough in his travel harness as we humans overdosed on adrenalin—we raced to Dad's third floor room, afraid to see him and still short on insight as to how to abort his impending doom. Tiptoeing through his open doorway, we were both discouraged and relieved to find him asleep; we'd counted on his lucidity and ingenuity to help us hatch a plan. But obviously his sleep was as important as our mission.

The nurses' station was right outside Dad's room and all was peaceful as one male nurse manned the computers. Here, at least, we were unknown, not the persona non grata we were over at skilled nursing. Here we were the concerned kin of the frail, traumatized, elderly gent in Room 303.

"Let's find out his status," I whispered to Lola and Chancy. "Everybody smile."

"Excuse me," we approached the nurse, "we came to visit Charlie in Room 303 — we're his daughters — but he's asleep and we don't want to wake him. Can you just update us on his status? I just flew in today from Hawai'i."

"Sure, let me just see what I have here." The kindly caregiver pulled up his computer pages, then scrolled for what he needed. "He's being released tomorrow morning," he told us, "on hospice."

An electric current ran through the three of us, while nothing was reflected on our faces. "Oh," I said pleasantly, "do you know what time?"

"No, it doesn't give a time." He glanced back at his screen. "Soon after breakfast would be my guess."

"Okay, thank you so much," we chorused, then moved casually away from his station, around a corner, and rapidly down a hall. The second we were out of earshot, we clutched ourselves into a big knot, staring incredulously into each other's faces, and hissing, "Tomorrow morning!" "Oh my God!" "What're we gonna do?!" "He's gonna die!" "What can we do?!"

We all agreed some sleep was in order. Tomorrow was almost here and we better rest up for…whatever. We had no playbook and we knew it. But we had each other. And I've rarely been as grateful for support and sisterhood as on that occasion.

I crawled into my Rodger-the-Lodger single bed in my cozy room with its warm duvet and owl-filled trees out in the night. I wanted to cry and pray and somehow come up with a scheme, but crises don't always afford such clarity. So White Boy (whose company I also cherished) and I just surrendered to hard-earned slumber.

And, wouldn't you know it, when I awoke at 5 a.m., an answer had come to me in the night. At 6, Lola phoned from where she was living an hour away. "I couldn't sleep all night," she said hurriedly. "I'm going back to the hospital right now."

"Me, too," I said. "I'll meet you there. And I have an idea."

"You do? What?"

"Tell you when we get there. I think you'll go for it."

"Great."

L'il White Boy had to stay behind in this big, cold house. Being Hawaiian, this chilly stuff was all new. But his near-death trials as a baby were still fresh enough that he fully trusted my behavior, inexplicable as it sometimes was.

Lola, Chancy, and I met in the hospital parking lot, where I unveiled the strategy the restful night had provided. We were highly charged by it, believing it might really work! Anxious to see how Dad was doing, we boogied up to his room. (Darlene was an early bird, but hopefully we'd beat her to the bedside.)

Dad was duly surprised to see me back from Hawai'i a mere two weeks after leaving him at The Shores. A thousand bucks a shot to get there is viewed as a statement of strong purpose. Plus, there were three of us today, visiting at 7 a.m.

"Well, well, well," he smiled, as we situated ourselves around him, "didn't expect to see you back so soon." He chuckled as I kissed his cheek, then looked quizzically from one to the other of us.

Without a second to waste, I began, "Dad, do you know what hospice is?"

"No. Should I?"

"No," we all said in unison, and everybody laughed.

"You don't wanna know what it is, Dad," I shook my head. "It's good you don't know." Lola and Chancy nodded. "Here's the thing though, you're supposed to be going to hospice today."

"TODAY," repeated Lola and Chancy.

"And…?" Dad pressed.

"…unless we get you out," said Lola. "And that's why we're here. We have a plan."

"Okay," said Dad, "I'm listening."

Now, I've had my moments with this guy through the decades, particularly in light of what seemed like either my wrong choices or his. However, we had a bond, spoken and unspoken, that ran deeper than any deed or misdeed either of us ever inflicted upon the other. In the most profound way, Dad knew that, in this moment, whatever Lola, Chancy, and I were up to, whatever the hell it might be, was in his best interest. He felt the electric current running through us and knew my return from Hawai'i wasn't whimsical or easy for me.

"What's the plan?" he was ready.

"Dad," I began, "take our word for it, you don't want to go to hospice. But it's been determined by your health proxy that you're supposed to go today."

"Okay, what do I need to do?"

"Well, there's only one person who can get you out."

"Who?" he asked, like a little elf who found this a fun guessing game.

"Who do you think?" I played along.

"The doctor?" he guessed.

"Nope," came the chorus of three.

Again he looked from one of us to the next. "Darlene?"

"Nope," we all shook our heads.

"You?" he raised his eyebrows toward me.

"Nope."

There was a silence. Who would he guess next?

"Then who?" he asked us, stumped.

"You!" We all pointed at him.

"Me?"

"Yup."

"Dad, are you of sound mind?" I asked.

"I believe I am."

"We believe you are, too," said Lola.

"And if you're of sound mind," I said, "you don't need a health proxy. A health proxy is only a back-up when a person can't make their own decisions. Are you capable of making your own health decisions?"

"I believe I am."

"We believe you are, too," Lola and I said together.

"So you have to do one thing, just one thing, but you have to do it right now. You ready? It's really easy." We were all leaning in toward him, ready to start the coaching.

"I'm ready."

"All you have to do is say to your doctor, `I don't want hospice.' Can you say that?"

He nodded slowly, still in the dark as to what hospice was, yet now convinced that the hallows of hell would be a frat party compared to it.

"Okay, repeat after me: I...don't...want...hospice," I enunciated.

He tried it, "I...don't...want...hostage."

"No-o-o," we all laughed, "not `hostage,' hospice."

"Try again: I don't want hospice."

He gave it another shot, "I...don't...want...hospage."

"No-o-o! C'mon, you gotta say it right." Everyone was laughing, including Dad, who had that enviable talent of finding lightness in the most dire straits and could probably cheer up Satan himself.

"Dad, here's the thing, you're going to be alone with the doctor and if you can't say the word right, he's going to think you're not of sound mind. Ya dig?"

"I dig."

"Okay, now try it again, `I don't want hospice.' It's really important that you say it right."

"*Really* important," said Lola and Chancy.

"I…don't…want…hospice," Dad said slowly.

"YAY!!" we cheered and bounced around. "Great! You said it!" Then we had him repeat it until we thought he'd mastered the word."

"Okay," I said, "I'm going to get Doctor Scheinbaum."

Lola had seen the wicked white-coated wonder walking past the doorway a short time earlier, so it looked like we could get the deed done right now.

"You guys practice a little more, and I'll go get him."

After our phone call, I didn't expect big hugs from the doc. So, in prep for this meeting, I'd dressed up a bit. It's harder to say no to a courteous, well-groomed lady than a dowdy, pouty bitch. I found the illusive fellow seated at a small desk right up the hall. He was working through some of the agonizing paperwork medical professionals are shackled with.

"Doctor Scheinbaum?"

"Yes?" He didn't look up from his papers, and continued scribbling.

"Doctor Scheinbaum?" He now lifted his head slightly, offering half a glance. "I'm Wendy, Charlie Raebeck's daughter. We spoke on the phone the other day."

"Yes?" He wasn't exactly basking in my charm.

"My father would like to talk to you."

"I'm too busy," he burrowed back into his pages. He wasn't going to look at me again.

Shucks, all dressed up and nowhere to go.

"Doctor Scheinbaum......my father is ninety years old, he's in a room right down the hall, he's your patient, and he wants to talk to you."

"Okay," he conceded, still without eye contact, "I'll talk to him, but only if he's the only person in the room."

"Oh, don't worry," I said breezily, "he'll be the only one in the room." (Like my shoes?)

"I'll be there in a minute," he muttered.

"Thank you," and I sped back to 303.

"He's coming!" I told the gang. "But he said Dad has to be alone! Are you ready, Dad? You know your line?"

"I'm ready," said Dad.

"He's ready," said Lola and Chancy. "Ready as he'll ever be." The Charlie Chaplin aspects of the scenario were not lost on any of us.

"Okay. Well, us three have to disappear. Bye, Dad...."

"Good luck," we all whispered, then moved out the door just as Shifty Scheinbaum entered, clipboard in hand, ignoring us completely.

We weren't entirely confident Dad's tongue would wrap properly around the new word, but the urgency combined with family love felt potent enough to carry the moment. As I've said, Dad was truly an alchemist in creating levity where there was none, and, despite the high stakes this morning, we were all actually having a jolly time.

From our post just outside Dad's doorway, where we locked our gaze on Scheinbaum as he approached the bedside, we crossed our fingers and even our ankles as we peeked around the doorjamb in suspense. The bed was partially draped, so only the back of the doc's smock and Dad's bundled feet under the covers could be seen. Probably we were nearer than Scheinbaum wished us, and definitely acting `like children,' but we weren't `in the room,' and couldn't help ourselves from straining to hear if Dad was performing as rehearsed. But, unfortunately, we weren't close enough to register the exchange.

Just moments later, the doctor turned from the bedside and headed toward us for the door. Now he was noting something on his clipboard. (More paperwork—poor thing.) As he approached the doorway, we three felt safe to re-enter. And as Scheinbaum passed me, he said aloud, while writing on his clipboard, "Patient does not want hospice at this time."

We waited a few ceremonious seconds for him to gain some distance from the room then the high fives, ecstatic jubilation, and grand congratulations filled the previously-clinical chamber. This was one fine family moment, not to mention something of a coup that I'd probably pay heavily for later. But Lola, Chancy, and I knew we'd saved Dad's life.

About thirty minutes into our merriment, Darlene bopped in, coiffed and slightly ruffled at the sight of us this early and this gleeful on what was set to be a somber day in Dad's life. She found it odd I was back so soon from so far, but wasn't one to indulge in trivia.

She sat on Dad's bedside. "How're you feeling?" she asked, pretending it was a normal day.

"Fine," he said cheerfully.

Electricity was crackling around the room now, as a short silence, probably the first one ever in our family, surfed the sound waves. Darlene glanced around, then back to her husband. "Did you have your breakfast?"

"No, not yet," said Dad, followed by another Chaplin-esque silence, that even Darlene seemed to notice.

Lola, never one for formalities, then blurted out, "Dad's not going to hospice, y'know, Darlene."

Taken aback, Darlene blinked. "Yes, he is," she said, looking from Lola over to me.

"No, he isn't," I said courteously.

Discombobulated, she then pivoted to Dad, "Yes, you are."

"No, I'm not," said Dad.

Darlene then leaned into him, as Scheinbaum might've done if we hadn't whipped him into shape, and said with chilling finality, "Yes, you are. Don't you remember, we talked about it last week? It's Comfort Care. You're. Not. Going. To. Get. Better."

An audible gasp escaped from the gallery. Then Dad, keeping his mild demeanor, looked straight at Darlene and said, "I'm absolutely not going."

Looking sharply around the room, Darlene then snapped to her feet like a switchblade and stormed out of the room without a word. She charged the nurses' station outside Dad's doorway to discern what major mishap could've sparked this snafu.

Back in 303, we four resumed our festivities. We were reasonably certain the laws, and even Scheinbaum, our new best friend, were on our side.

And soon it was determined that dear Dad was to be transported back to The Shores. Knowing that Darlene, her two sons, and my brothers (and all the boys' wives) were expecting the happy hospice folk to commence their work, we three prepared for a full day of…whatever we had to do to hold our ground.

We really didn't have much of a 'mob' at this point. Our other two sympathetic sisters were in Virginia and Idaho.

"I'll go get Isabelle," I told Lola, knowing that this seventy-year-old friend (from way, way back in the pre-

Darlene days) would do anything for our clan, particularly if I served as chauffeur. I'd have to drive ninety minutes each way to collect her and return her home later, but we'd then have four guardians—or Charlie's Angels, as we named ourselves. And the sight of the beloved and adorably French Isabelle might calm some of the family feathers expected to bristle later today, as word got out that Dad had slipped through the cracks.

"See you at The Shores," I told Lola and Chancy, and zoomed off in Isabelle's direction.

Darling Isabelle, truly valued by our tribe and somewhat lost to us after our mother had died decades earlier, was the icing on our coup. At The Shores, we four positioned ourselves squarely around Charlie's bed, as the fated hospice day unfolded. And we remained there as sentinels until the sun went down.

In the first few hours and throughout the afternoon, the rest of the family, who drifted in throughout the day, peeked into the room for a quick nod to Dad or to simply observe us all holding court. At times, they were literally huddled out in the hallway, seemingly at an impasse as to what to do or say. At one point, one of my brothers stepped into the room, took in the conviviality, then whispered in my ear, as if letting me in on the news, "Dad's not going to hospice."

But the entire day, not only did no one from hospice ever appear, not only was it basically business as usual at The Shores with all Dad's nurse friends delighted to have him back, but no relatives, none, had a word to say to any of us, nor any questions. They kept their distance all day long while convening nervously outside the room.

Not only that, but ever thereafter, and to this day, there has never been a word spoken or asked by those family members regarding how and why Dad was excused from hospice. In fact, about three years later, I mentioned to my other brother, "Don't you want to know how come Dad never went to hospice and what happened?"

"I do want to know," he answered, "but some other time, not now." And I knew not to bring it up again.

So Scheinbaum's prophesy did not come to pass. His "two months, three at the most" expiration date came and went. In fact, sixty-six months passed after that unholy prediction. And although bedridden and confined to a wheelchair thereafter, Dad (star patient at The Shores, revered by all) taught everyone priceless lessons about being of good cheer regardless of any and all circumstance.

Twice after hospice day, wishing to jog his memory, I recounted to him what had taken place. But the whole ordeal, from Stony Brook Hospital to the local one, and all that transpired during that drugged-up time lasting several months in all, were forgotten to him. And as I told the tale, he listened wide-eyed in bed like a child to a bedtime story. I knew on some visceral plane, in his heart or his sinews, the story hit home—because he was fully awake living it right beside Charlie's Angels—but he either forgot it all or chose to. And both times after I told the tale, he said at the end, "That's a good story, you should write it down."

That was December 2011. It's now November 2017. Dad made it to ninety-five and a half. He remained bedridden because he couldn't regain enough muscle strength in his legs since his insurance only covered three hours a week of physical therapy (and I, of course, was benched and silenced). But one of my step-brothers bought him a motorized wheelchair. And Darlene stayed by his side, dedicated and devoted to him every single day for the next five and a half years.

The local family members let Dad heal in his own way after hospice day. And though no one speaks of it, I think we're a better family now.

Nutrition and holistic health aren't yet embraced by the medical community but at least these days patients aren't force-fed Sprite anymore. Dad talked his way off most of his prescriptions once his caregivers grew to love and believe in him. And he was down to only two daily pills the last few years.

Unfortunately, an incident placed dear Charlie back in that damn hospital bed. Shiny Scheinbaum was on hand once again. I never saw him, but knew he'd eaten his words many, many moons ago. And good old Dad only suffered twenty-four hours that last time. Surrounded and tenderly assisted by the family members who lived nearby, he died five minutes after my plane landed at JFK.

Precious Dad, coolest of the cool.

LITTLE CLOWN

I was six, Leslie was seven, but we looked like twins. Oma, Mom's mother, who always wanted more granny time, hang the cost, hatched a plan: Mom could concentrate on the younger kids while Leslie and I took our first plane-ride, then summered at the seashore. Oma would have us to herself for two weeks.

We two would fly alone from Memphis to New York City to meet her. (Fly? Alone?) But once Mom convinced us that the expedition, hardly the norm in 1956, was a Grand Opportunity, we shelved our hesitancy. And everyone thereafter who got wind of our upcoming launch, commended us on our bravery and marveled at what splendid fortune had befallen such pipsqueaks.

Soon into the arrangements, Dad's mother, also a New Yorker, learned that grandchildren were being trafficked right past her without a word. Phone calls to Oma followed; the plan would have to be re-worked. Oma fought for control and every sort of leverage—she was, after all, paying the airfare—but Grandma deserved equal time.

Things grew awkward. Oma had lived across the street from us back in North Carolina and was not only far more familiar to us than Grandma, but an everyday Mrs. Claus.

She knew what kids liked; goodies seemed to grow from her hands. Grandma, on the other hand, unlike the candy-meister, seemed austere, and we hardly knew her.

"The new plan," Mom announced, "is that you'll fly to New York, Oma will meet your plane, take you to Wildwood Beach for a week, then Grandma will come and spend the second week there with you. You two will stay right at the same hotel and Grandma will get there before Oma leaves."

"But we don't *want* to be with Grandma, we only want to be with Oma."

"You hardly even know Grandma. How do you know you won't have a good time?"

"We know."

"You'll have a fine time with both of them, you'll see. You'll be at the beach, you'll be staying in a hotel! It's going to be a wonderful trip. They both love you and want very much to have some time with you. Give Grandma a chance."

That sort of forced, upbeat explanation proves that a mother's mind is made up. Fairness had won the day and we were to grasp the principle. Oma would have to grasp it, too.

Departure day arrived. The huge propeller plane rolled to a stop on the tarmac at Memphis Airport. A staircase magically spilled from its side, and both Mom and Dad walked us across the pavement and all the way onto the plane for a parental pow-wow with the smooth, stockinged stewardesses with upside-down rowboat hats curved around their hairdos. These were like magazine ladies, and being under their spell for three hours would be like eating banana cream pie. Not to mention the cool airplane interior, everything spanking new, orderly, and compact. We instantly got why everyone was so thrilled for us.

In flight, we were on excellent behavior — default mode around unfamiliar adults. That and the matching dresses Oma had made won us constant attention and all sorts of treats. "Traveling alone to New York!"

Everything went exactly as Mom had outlined. We quickly felt like world travelers, awed by the ease of this flying-to-New-York thing. You sit down, you gape out the window, you eat a fancy meal, have some cocoa, talk with the pretty ladies, and presto you're there! And Leslie was an exemplary companion — older and bent on decorum, lest we be graded after the flight. Her etiquette, mimicked by the tomboy twin, won rave reviews on the ground as Oma met the plane. We were A+ passengers, welcome again on Pan American Airlines any old time.

From the moment we landed, I was pretty much just along for the ride. Questions I had were quietly posed to Big Sis, often a step ahead of me in gleaning why we were doing this or that. She better understood that when you're out of your element, being a good dog is recommended. (And good behavior was pretty easy since the entire adventure was tailored to delight us.)

We spent a day in Oma's Upper East Side apartment. A total Kraut, she had made her home in 'German Town,' a few square blocks of German pastry shops, German sausage shops, and German people. In fact, Oma's lifestyle was so completely Deutsch that Mom had to correct me when I later told people I'd been to Germany over the summer.

After Germany, we bused to the Jersey Shore. Now this was livin'! At night, the boardwalk bustled with every imaginable ride and booths bursting with stuffed animals. Pink cotton candy spun out of machines onto sticks and all over our faces. In the daytime, the white sand beach was covered in bright umbrellas and families in stripes. Every good thing about the 1950's — innocence, safety, ease, loose dogs, and blue waves rolling to shore. Plus two little girls in matching swim suits designed and stitched by Oma.

Upon arrival at the beach each day, Oma had us build her a sand dais to sit upon. Poised in her summer frock, she'd watch for hours as we frolicked in the shorebreak. No parents to scold us, no resistance from anywhere, just this lenient chaperone. With the Queen of Yes, there were lunches and ice creams, then back to the fancy hotel for dinner before a jaunt along the promenade. Oma thrived on our glee, seeing it her duty to indulge us. She had literally saved her nickels and dimes for this.

All three of us were blue to see the week's conclusion. But, as promised, one morning we went to meet Grandma's bus, and that afternoon Oma boarded another and waved her white hanky at us through the window as it pulled away.

Grandma was grateful to commence her time-share, but the tone of our holiday instantly shifted. This new guardian was sedate, stern, and proper. Where Oma was spendy, Grandma was not, "You went to the boardwalk every night?" Grandma believed spoiling children would ruin them for life. "You had cotton candy every night?"

But Grandma had brought us each a gift that she presented as she unpacked her suitcase. Since we customarily weren't spoiled, the two beautifully wrapped boxes were exciting. And store-bought. (Nothing from homemaker Oma was ever store-bought.) "Open them," invited Grandma. So we carefully undressed the bows and paper, each finding ourself holding a small white box the size of an adult's hand. Grandma looked on as we lifted the lids. It meant a lot to her that we like what she brought us; her competition was fierce.

Inside my box was a bright fuchsia bean-bag clown. Fastidiously sewn by hand, he had an embroidered face and real-looking curly black hair. A cute smile was stitched onto his white face along with happy half-moon eyes. At the neck, he wore layers of white mesh ruffles, and below were felt hands and beet-colored cloth over his bean legs. A portrait of refinery, he was tickled to have the box opened by a little girl. Leslie, simultaneously, opened her box to find an identical clown with turquoise legs.

Still high on the fumes of Oma, we didn't know what to make of these clowns. We thanked Grandma—clearly she'd gone out of her way to get them—but were secretly confounded as to what one does with such things. Were they toys? Not really, too nice. The European, mime-like look on their faces suggested they sit on a mantel or live in a glass case, not be cast about the playground.

"Do you each like the color of your clown?" Grandma asked, "or do you want to switch?" She wasn't around enough to know that Leslie traditionally got the pink and I the blue. As the oldest, Leslie declared first dibs and always chose pink because she was a girl. I, apparently the `boy,' learned young that Leslie wasn't to be crossed. ("I'm a girl, too" had gotten me nowhere.) Thankfully, blue was a fantastic color—that I pretended to hate so Leslie wouldn't get any ideas.

She'd probably want the pink clown now—she never ever took blue. But, perhaps because she didn't care, or maybe out of politeness to Grandma, Leslie kept the blue this time, and I the pink. I truly had never had pink anything, so the color was novel.

We masked our sentiments about these prissy clowns but they were another harbinger that the week ahead would be a downgrade.

But Grandma had been up against Oma for a while now and wasn't fazed. She kept us fed, bathed, and beached, but every night at the boardwalk? Ludicrous. And cotton candy will rot your teeth. So we played cards at the hotel at night and tried to be gracious grandchildren. Grandma came out the pronounced loser of the trip—too strict and serious, and not much fun compared to her rival. And she must have felt challenged by the situation. Fairness did not rule the day after all.

Nothing happened with the clowns. They were a nice gesture from Grandma, but we never played with them and rarely mentioned them again. (In fact, later in life, Leslie had no recollection of them.) Back in Memphis, we showed them to Mom and Dad. Seeing our shrugs, Mom suggested they were maybe too mature a present for our ages; we might appreciate them more later on. They were quite nice, she said, but not exactly toys. Still, Mom was right, we'd had an exciting trip.

I kept my clown in his box for a long time. Whenever I peeked inside, often with that lasting inner query as to what I was meant to do with him, I was repeatedly impressed at how intricately he was made, how cheery he remained, and how he always seemed ready to begin with me. When we moved from Memphis to Chicago and then to Ohio, I kept him as a distant relative of the fuzzy menagerie that occupied my bed. He stayed in his box, usually in a closet. Leslie had hers stashed somewhere, too.

After a number of years, it was apparent the little clown had passed some endurance test. Teddy and the others had slipped away with grade school, but the clown, who never got a name, stayed alert and cute with his white ruffles, fine hair, and pink pantaloons. By then we lived on Long Island and had long understood our two opposite grannies, Oma continuing to sponsor every indulgence while Grandma would quietly drink hot water for breakfast on her rare visits.

Grandma died first at eighty-four. Then Mom at forty-five. And finally Oma at eighty-six. The little clown, now out of his box and usually in full view somewhere in my room, was something old, something from them, even something of me and my "twin" (who was now anything but), something from that first foray from the nest, that summer with the grandmothers when we learned to fly. Maybe his pinkness recalled some subconscious liberation.

I went to college briefly, then lived in various European and American cities as I found my way to adulthood. The little clown with his cheerful countenance, now a relic of my childhood, greeted me when I'd periodically rummage through possessions in Dad's shed. "Oh, the little clown," I'd murmur, "he's still here." He always took me by surprise, as clowns do. His pink bean-bag legs were fading now and one day a hole appeared in the seam and a few beans rolled out. It stunned me that twenty years had passed and the beans were still good. But it wasn't right to see his innards. I popped them back inside him and patched the seam. And though the little guy was fraying at the edges and his ruffles weren't as crisp, his sweet face shone as brightly as that first day in Wildwood.

He was a keeper. But with another couple of decades he was aging. The pantaloons wore thin, beans spilled out here and there when I lifted him up. I had to retire him to the safety of a quiet drawer or find a safe nest on a high shelf. He mustn't be disturbed—he had become important and fragile.

When I moved to Hawai'i, things got rough. The clown was fifty now. Tropical insects, I was to learn, stop at nothing—including ancient beans. I realized after the first year that the clown's insides were slowly being eaten! Now, to save his life, he was forced to dwell in the freezer! There, in a plastic bag, he was chilly but at least safe. He lived there for several years and, even then, never held a grudge.

Then it was back to the Mainland, to Long Island winters and occasional drama, as Dad reached his nineties. I rented a room next door to the retirement community where he and my step-mother lived. And just yesterday, as I packed up to return to Hawai'i, where property and work now demanded attention, I found my little clown one more time. He'd been living in a parked car on Long Island for seven straight months (along with all my East Coast stuff), pushed aside like everything in my world as I fought to spend time with Dad against practical odds. Unpacked from the car, the tarnished little clown seemed to ask me what had happened. Were we letting everything go? His beans were all over the place, and I carefully put them back inside his tattered pink legs. "Is it all falling apart?" he wondered, without registering any trace of a frown.

No, my little clown. No, not at all. You're still my sweet mascot of joy and endurance. My thought then was to take him to see Dad, now bed-ridden in a nursing facility for a solid year, and to tell Dad how this gift from his mother had miraculously accompanied me through half a century. But I had to pack things up instead, including my beat-up friend.

So I pressed him snugly into himself with utmost care, so the beans would stay put till I had more time. I wrapped him in a blue silk handkerchief I bought in Thailand, making everything soft around him. And finally I placed him in plastic against the cold or mold or anything that might invade a parked car in December.

I'd be back in a month. And I knew my little clown understood that Dad came first right now. Yet tonight the clown seemed not unlike Dad — two small frail ones who've been with me always, smiling all the way, constantly surprising me with their unquenchable joy.

And Dad's mother gave me both. Maybe in her stern way, Grandma gave Dad his inner resources, too. Maybe she knew the value of what's quiet and meaningful and enduring. Maybe Grandma, Dad, and the little clown are the tortoises, not the hares, of this world, and maybe it takes a lifetime to appreciate what they know and teach.

But whoever would have guessed, that day Leslie and I unwrapped the boxes and stared uncertainly at the new clowns, that fifty-six years down the road mine would have won my heart completely and become my oldest keepsake, a precious link to two generations long gone, and the last artifact of that summer we found our wings.

✳ ✳ ✳

And, as a postscript, with Leslie now gone, too, my fading little clown links me to three generations, and……my childhood twin.

VINTAGE SNAPSHOTS

Falling in love with a place can be a romance lasting years, decades, even forever. Talk about unconditional love—places don't demand loyalty; you can have them your way and the highway. Sometimes it's love at first sight, sometimes they grow on you, sometimes you never get to find out what might've been. There are favorite places, places with weird vibes, places you can't forget, and places that make you feel out of place. Even a long life of travel leaves a zillion places undiscovered.

The United States, for all her weakness and new-fangled confusion, still boasts a geography bar none. To set out on a 3000-mile trip without even a passport, and driving one's own car, is a phenomenal entitlement we Yanks really take for granted. Every country has its magnificence and unmatched landscape and temperament, but the U.S. is freakin' glorious, staggeringly abundant, unsurpassed in variety, and fabulously accessible.

It had been much too long; I couldn't even remember the last time I'd driven coast to coast. It's hard to swing it though. To drive round-trip, you need time, money, and stamina; but if you do one-way, your car ends up stuck on the wrong end of the continent. I hate that. Still, I found myself jonesin' for the Midwest, of all places—the fields and farmers, the Heartland. I didn't have roots there or friends, just felt disconnected from Middle America. The Dust Bowl, the Corn Belt, the Bible Belt didn't really exist for me; I was always flying over, never touching down.

It was there and in the deep South, on back roads, where you'd come upon rickety pick-up trucks with rickety drivers in straw hats and overalls. Honest smiles with missing teeth. Waggy-tail dogs with waggy-tail kids. Haystacks. Where a pitch-fork wasn't a Hollywood prop. I was hankerin' for rustic, uncombed, unselfconscious, unkempt. I had the vision of a faded navy blue 1949 pick-up with a loose back fender and kids with freckles and unruly cowlicks wedged in amongst their wooden table and chairs and everything the truck could hold as they drove too slowly down a two-lane highway. On their faces you could see all they'd left behind, as well as the glimmer of hope about where they were headed. The kids would wave if you were in the car behind them.

I'd always found vivid local color on cross-country rambles. There had been five previously, yet I'd hardly scratched the surface of these awesome States. I learned early to avoid the freeways completely, that the smaller roads yielded not only every amenity, but scenery, out-of-the-way hamlets, and the folks I was looking for.

Now it was January 2013, I was sixty-two, and somehow thirty-six years had lapsed since my last coast-to-coast. The mission this time was straight-forward. I had to get my 1999 Saab from Eastern Long Island to my empty carport in Venice, California, where I maintained a small apartment. The building had fifteen units but only fourteen carports. For that reason, I couldn't 'hold' an empty carport for future use. Use it or lose it, I had been warned.

Meanwhile, the Saab was sitting under a New York snowdrift. My tenure on Long Island—an attempt to live next door to my aging father—had proven financially hilarious, and had now reached its term. So I had to either sell the car and modest household possessions or get them all to the West Coast. I'd put thousands into the Saab at that point, so it seemed smarter to keep it than start over with an unknown entity.

Now…there are plenty who would choose another time of year to take the back roads through the Rockies. But after living in Hawai'i for ten years and Southern California for twenty before that, I'd come to cherish January's cold whiteness. It chases people indoors, leaving nature bold and unattended, stark like black and white photography. And, having done my time in cold places, I knew insulated attire is key, so I wouldn't be unprepared.

There are also many who'd go to extremes to avoid having their cat riding shotgun on a cross-country cruise. But White Boy was roadworthy, hardy, and a good sport. In his one and a half years, he'd already flown from Kaua'i to O'ahu to New York, then back to LA. And he'd now been exiled there six long months while getting shots and paperwork to return to his Hawaiian homeland. Moving vehicles aren't exactly a preferred feline habitat, but we two needed to be together after his string of questionable catsitters. (When all else fails, become a petsitter?) Besides, I sorely missed my little straight-man; his presence on this trip would be anything but a hindrance. So, although flying one's cat three thousand miles in order to then drive him back to the starting point may sound ill-conceived, loved ones sometimes need to reunite. So on my way from Kaua'i to NY, I'd stop in LA to collect the fluff-ball. All I had to do then was conceal him in a motel for a few nights while spending Christmas with Dad on Long Island, then, America, here we come!

By the time we were set to sail — the buggy packed with baskets, blankets, boxes, and comfy perches for cat naps — I had fully overridden the recurring comment from those hip to my plan, "What if the Saab breaks down in the middle of Kansas?"

I mean, imagine being governed by concerns like that? I'd have died of boredom at age ten. "If the car breaks down, I guess we'll deal with it."

So, with the car and the cat as white as the plentiful snow, we chugged west, anxious to leave the East Coast and expensive motels in our wake. And it was with mild annoyance that I realized the first day out, that I'd been had — paying $650 to repair the heater. It emitted a tepid airflow no more than twenty degrees warmer than what was smacking the windshield, and never warm enough to remove woolly hat, mittens, ski jacket, or scarf. 'Snowman' would be my new look. But at least it made hopping in and out of the sixteen-degree weather less of an ordeal. But the cold wasn't a concern for White Boy, an exotic specimen with show-cat long white hair and cerulean blue eyes, who wasn't exactly purring over this space capsule to Mars. Yet — as he had from the day I rescued him from certain death at four weeks old — he placed total trust in his unpredictable parent.

Though this was my sixth drive across, I'd never done it without another human, nor with such liberty of time. But White Boy and I truly were in no rush. (Well, actually he was, but I wasn't.) Who knew when we'd have the opportunity again, might as well milk it; traveling slow or fast, we'd use the same amount of gas. And a few more motels would only cost $40-50 a night — worth it in the greater scheme of travel and adventure.

We were just pining for Kentucky, Missouri, Kansas… and of course Colorado and Utah! We had even hoped to visit a girlfriend (of mine, not his) who'd relocated to North Dakota. Would be great to see a buddy and finally those crazy Dakotas that just never seem to get any closer. But blizzards were swirling up north as we sallied west. And freezing to death by the side of the road is harder to take in stride than breaking down in Kansas. Plus, we could lose days and days should we get snowed in up there, so we couldn't chance it. Anyway, how can you break down in Kansas if you don't go to Kansas?

So we went to Kansas and, sure enough, had our break-down. Of course no one had the foreign fuel pump we needed, but White Boy and I dealt with it. In fact, we got to spend two extra days in a tiny town in the Midwest, just what we wanted.

It was a fine journey. When you're on a road trip, time stops completely. Your vehicle is your home, the coiling pavement and map are your world, along with your companion and the stops you make. Fields and mountains, rivers and livestock, motels and odd meals, snow and ice. You're traveling, you're on the move; you're sort of alone out there, yet there are plenty of other cross-country pilgrims, truckers, people relocating, and traveling salesmen.

But on the back roads, the traffic's more regional. And it was weird, therefore, that we didn't see anyone smacking of local color. And it wasn't just the time of year; local color didn't seem to exist anymore. There were no old pick-up trucks. None. We saw some elderly folks who very likely were or had been farmers, but they drove shiny new pick-ups. They wore new overalls. And we didn't see them by the side of the road fixing a flat, we saw them parking at malls. If anyone was moving all their earthly possessions, they probably rented a U-Haul and took the freeways as fast as possible to their new home. We didn't see any scruffy kids with big burly dogs. We saw a few smaller breeds in the front seats of four-wheel-drive Chevys, with their groomed owners in new hats and clean gloves. No one had an old car. No one. No one seemed to be living a rustic or sketchy life. There wasn't a pitch-fork or haystack in sight, and I was actually quite disappointed. Everyone had nice teeth, though they weren't grinning like they used to.

White Boy didn't have much to compare this odyssey to, so I couldn't share these observations with him, but he remained a diehard sidekick through sleet and snow, cold and even colder, as he eventually chose the center back window as his sweet spot in our mobile unit. He also, almost audibly, wondered if this was going to be a permanent way of life for us. He'd endured nothing but change in his existence thus far, now he was sampling twelve new states in twenty-one days. What next?

Yeah, it was kind of a sad day when I realized that what I'd been yearning for was a time not a place. The past. What I'd sought on this trip, aside from the glories of the natural world, was gone forever. 1949 pick-up trucks are pricey antiques now. Giant machines pitch hay or shovel it into stacks. And farmers are solvent businessmen with macho four-wheelers and probably some debt. And those without teeth are now more likely to be city-dwellers—homeless or buried under false American dreams somewhere. Everyone at the shopping centers in the Midwest, and everywhere for that matter, was going about their business in that generic American way we've come to accept.

It's okay. I still had the Rockies ahead in Colorado, and then the ecstasy of Southern Utah's national parks. But the Midwest didn't quite deliver.

Then, after the Kansas breakdown, as we were stocking up on food at a grocery store at mall #812, I walked back across the snowy parking lot to the old white Saab, not exactly hard to spot among the rows of identical new cars and trucks. There, White Boy waited in the rear window, amidst the neatly-stacked cargo. With my woolly cap down to my eyes and scarf up over my nose, I wasn't exactly stylin' as I climbed behind the wheel. Then again, who'd ever notice, in the middle of winter in the middle of Kansas?

That's when I saw two teenage girls in the car parked opposite us. Not only did they notice, but they were taking pictures of this odd-looking vehicle—unknown in these parts—white in the snow, with the fluffy white cat in the back window. And they were giggling.

"White Boy's pretty cute in that back window," I chuckled. Until I realized the whole picture, through their young eyes: I was the kooky older lady, dressed for an Arctic expedition, traveling who knows where with my cat and all my possessions, in an old, unidentifiable car with New York plates. I was the story, the not-so-local color. I was their cool photograph. As true as anything could be, I was the quirky image they stumbled upon, that I myself couldn't find. The salt of the earth, wayward soul making her way to some new place with her whole life in tow. At least to them.

I kind of wanted to say, "It's not as bad as it looks, we live in Hawai'i, we actually have another car, and we're kind of just seeing the sights out here." But that would've ruined what they were seeing, so I pretended not to notice them. And I'm glad they got that snapshot—it was a goody.

LOVE AND PEACE

Journalism and I were a natural pairing. Even now, twenty-two years since my last article, I'm intrigued almost daily by news stories all over the globe that I'd love to cover. "But I have a cat," I conclude, "and I live in Hawai'i."

But if you're raised to be opinionated, if writing is a default pastime, and if you're both curious and suspicious, what could be more rewarding than to travel (with a press pass to open every door) to some unfolding story that reeks of greed and injustice, track down key people, get the dirt, and then publish your report for all to read?

Quite satisfying really.

If you want to choose and pitch your own stories, though, rather than be a staffer on assignment, then you're a freelancer. And freelance anything falls under the `starving artist' banner. So you won't be living large, and you'll pay your own airfare. For an artiste, however, the `free' part of `freelance' is what lets you select stories you believe should be told.

Once I found a few editors appreciative of my viewpoint and capabilities, it wasn't hard to get green lights and deadlines for stories. Not as lucrative or prestigious as being a staff writer, but while I was free-ranging, the well-heeled herd was thundering off en masse (under lavish expense accounts) to the next breaking headliner, to write cookie-cutter stories.

So I worked on my own time, wrote about what compelled me and, when not off in the field, spent long mornings scrawling in a corner cafe on Venice Boardwalk. That was around 1985, before cafe tables became internet cubicles. Cafes, back then, were the most European element of American life, and jovial hubs for new or familiar faces to meet the day and pass conversational tidbits across lattes and croissants.

Both the espresso and the ambience aided my productivity, so I was a regular. This establishment was commandeered by Gino, a sculpted body-builder from the Island of Malta, who was so unassuming and non-proprietary that it was a year before I realized he owned the joint. The oceanfront setting attracted the entire world to imbibe there, particularly after 11 a.m., at which time we locals vanished until tomorrow, but the mornings were ours. And whether on roller-skates, salty from the waves, with or without bicycles, or sometimes even in our city clothes, we spent hours gazing out to sea, removed momentarily from responsibility.

A few months into my tenure at the cafe, I noticed an outrageously handsome man who clearly knew Gino well. Considering this customer's cheekbones, confidence, and casual good taste, I decided he was someone to pointedly ignore.

Being unnoticed by women probably wasn't something he'd experiencecd. Especially unaccompanied ones, month after month, in a folksy setting like this.

Over time, we were both fixtures in the morning scene—sometimes at the sidewalk tables, sometimes inside.

His voice grew familiar to me and, wouldn't you know it, a buttery French accent topped off his profile. Added incentive to remain engrossed in my work.

Then one day after several months, the smooth foreigner, coffee in hand, slid into the empty chair opposite me. "May I join you?" he asked.

"Ok." I was hardly annoyed by the interruption.

"You're always writing," he said. "Are you working on a book?"

"No, newspaper articles."

"Oh. About what?"

"Different stuff. This one's about the homeless encampments on the beach."

"What uzzer things have you written about?"

"Oh, off-shore drilling, socially conscious investing, the Contra War in Nicaragua, nuclear testing in the Nevada desert, Ralph Nader, mostly political stuff."

"And what do you say about zese things?"

"I just write the truth. Try to help people understand that what `The New York Times' or Ronald Reagan say isn't necessarily factual. And if there's another side to an issue, like the environmental or human rights perspective, I want to show it. I try to make my articles more educational than political, but I'm a bit disgusted with Washington right now. Like, all these homeless people on the beach—they weren't here two years ago. They're the result of Reagan cutting welfare programs. Don't get me started. I mean, America was never like this before. We never had people living on the streets."

The dark-haired, dark-eyed man, introducing himself as Antoine, agreed with me on all of this, but didn't ebulliently share my determination to help or save my country. He was not only European, but had only lived in the U.S. a few years, and before that had literally circled the globe, spending months and years in Bali, Japan, New Zealand, and other longitudes where American issues didn't predominate. His viewpoint wasn't necessarily broader, but he lacked ownership in the Stars and Stripes. Or perhaps this was just another stop on his journey.

From that day forward, Antoine always sat at my table. And after a few more months, we'd join each other, always by chance, nearly every day and banter for hours — light-hearted, sidewalk philosophy. His ancestry, it turned out, wasn't strictly French (from the Mediterranean island of Corsica); he had a Moorish grandmother from Morocco, thus distancing him even more from my American 1950's upbringing, and adding a layer to his outlook.

Like, when our table was approached by a homeless person on the boardwalk begging for coins or food, a daily event we all were somewhat inured to, and the patrons would pause and reflect uncomfortably as the tattered person moved amongst the tables. "Sometimes you give, sometimes you don't," Antoine said lightly. "But zey want you to believe that giving to zem makes you a good person."

"What do you mean?"

"Giving money to the homeless isn't what makes you a good person," he shrugged. "You should already know whether you're good or not. But most pipple aren't sure, so zey give in order to believe zey are."

"You think so?"

"Yes. And the homeless understand zat's what's 'appening."

"Really?"

"Of course, zat's why it works. But you don't give zem money to be good. Giving to street pipple is a mood thing — sometimes you feel like it, sometimes you don't. It has nuzzing to do wiz whether you're a good person or not."

The attraction was obviously mutual. But on two occasions, Antoine told me I reminded him of his ex-wife, in both looks and personality. "You're too much like her," he'd say, "and it didn't work out wiz us. We got divorced."

"What happened?" I asked each time.

"She loved nature and ze country, so we moved to a horse ranch outside of Pasadena. That's what made her 'appy. But I got so-o bored out zere. I mean, we got to the point where we would just stay home at night and watch TV. Can you imagine? Zat's when I knew it was over—we were going to watch TV every night for the rest of our lives?"

I had to giggle, he made it sound so agonizing. "Well, I don't watch TV. I don't even have a TV."

"She didn't either when we started out. But she wanted to be in ze country. She loved animals and nature. And I do, too, but I can't live like ZAT."

Antoine seemed convinced a relationship with me was doomed. And I really couldn't present a strong case to the contrary. Thus, it always seemed right to just end our lovely mornings with, "Nice chatting with you" or "See you soon." Still, it might be nice to at least have dinner....

And then one day, Antoine took me to see a house in Santa Monica that he was considering buying. It was the first time we'd left the cafe. I approved of the house, of course, but it was never mentioned again.

And another surprise ensued when he told me his parents were visiting from Europe and invited me to have lunch with them. This occasion was an all-around smash because I was totally smitten by these elders—a class act of parentage—and Antoine was flabbergasted to learn I spoke French. Somehow it had never come up before. (And for the next few days, he'd just stare at me over coffee and say, "I can't believe you speak French. Why didn't you tell me?" And I'd just laugh.)

I had more than a crush on Antoine. We got to know each other well in that limited arena. But we almost never took it outside the cafe. We rarely touched. We never kissed. I don't think we ever spoke on the phone. "We look good togezzer," he said a couple of times, almost as a suggestion. But the ex-wife comparison seemed to haunt him.

I found in Antoine much that I sought in a man. Except for one little flaw: he was a night bird. He partied at the discos and danced the nights away. He spent money and befriended the ladies. Such was his life. At thirty-six, I was no homebody, but noise, smoke, drinking, late nights, and the close proximity of gyrating bodies had less appeal to me.

He was a photographer, and I recall asking once for his help with some photos. I remember bringing sheets of slides to his apartment (that he shared with Gino, it turned out) and Antoine helping me select the best ones, or something to that effect. Then, in reciprocation, I invited him over for homemade lasagna. But we hadn't confirmed which evening it would be, and then it rained hard a few days and we didn't see each other. I remember blubbering some weak apology to Gino in the cafe to pass on to Antoine since I didn't have his number. But the dinner never happened. Truth was, I was terrified of being alone with him at night. We would've become lovers, how could we not? Then we'd have married, moved back to that horse ranch in Pasadena, and soon divorced. It was just as well the lasagna got rained out.

Antoine inadvertently gave me something memorable, though. One morning, I was writing at an inside cafe table, and the smooth Frenchman cheerily took his seat across from me. "So what are we fighting today?" he smiled at the handwritten pages splayed across the table.

I frowned. "I'm not fighting," I said defensively, "I'm just writing......the truth. I'm not a fighter."

"You're not fighting wiz weapons, but you're fighting."

There was something in that moment....

I'd spent my life promoting peace, protesting the Vietnam War, marching for civil rights starting at age nine with my father in Columbus, Ohio. I was someone for whom the hippie movement was a custom fit; I'd already subscribed to the whole package, and truly believed then that the world was going to change and peace was on the way—we just had a lot of work to do. But it was all about peace; fighting was the worst thing you could do. And that was the purpose of writing these articles, to bring about peace.

"Do you really see me that way?" I stared at Antoine, who just laughed.

But this comment, this morning, from this man who I had come to adore, set me back a few paces. I couldn't stop thinking, "He sees me as a fighter. Am I a fighter?" The very word had such stigma in my world.

Walking home from the cafe that morning, I passed a palmist on Venice Boardwalk. "Palm Reading—only five dollars!" she sang out.

Five dollars, hey, why not? "Okay," I sat down in her little client chair.

"Make a fist," she started out, "and grip your thumb inside the fist with your other fingers."

I did that.

"Now squeeze the fist tight and hold it toward me."

I squeezed my fingers into a fist with the thumb tucked in and held the hand toward her. With her index finger, she tapped on the flesh between the base of my thumb and the base of my own index finger. I had no idea what she was up to. Then she did it again and looked at me. "Oooh, you're a fighter," she said.

I looked at her, surely unable to conceal my dismay. Thanks a lot, lady.

"When that flesh right there is hard," she said, "that means you're a fighter, and yours is really hard." She tapped it again as proof.

I wasn't thrilled with this reading, and forgot all of it quite soon, except that first part.... It was just too strange to be called a fighter by two different people the same morning, and for the first time in my entire life.

But I thought about it. And realized that I was a fighter. I realized that my passions about so many issues were fueled by not just a sense of being right where others were wrong, but a dislike, an overt condescension for those others. And thinking on it from this perspective, maybe the outlook Antoine had—that might also be taken for apathy or not caring enough—it didn't seem feasible to *fight* for *peace*. It seemed almost comical, in fact. An impossibility. Yet that's what I'd been doing. Fighting quite hard, with sincere animosity for those I was fighting. I called myself peaceful, and `believed' in peace; but I wasn't peaceful, I was a fighter.

And I recalled clearly something an old, apolitical friend had said years earlier, "I don't vote because politics breeds hatred." I'd disputed him at the time. But he hadn't budged in his conviction, and now I finally understood it.

Maybe I took Antoine's comment too seriously because I so appreciated his philosophy, his conversation, and company. Maybe I overreacted....

But I don't think so. Nor was it mere coincidence that the palmist backed up his statement that same damn day.

I stopped fighting after that. Stopped cold in my tracks. Never wrote another controversial newspaper article—pointing the finger at the bad guys and implying that I was somehow better. That's not peace. You can't fight for peace.

You have to be peaceful for peace. You can educate, you can protest, you can boycott, you can vote, you can take a stand, you can share information, you can change your lifestyle, you can research, you can unveil, you can even expose...but you have to be peaceful for peace. Otherwise you're just greasing the same big machine you're afraid of. You're playing the same game. The game of hatred. You're polarizing, you're insulting, you're building fences, not bridges.

Several years later, after the mild-mannered Gino had sold his stake in the cafe, he was killed in a motorcycle crash late one night up on Mulholland Drive. It was really, really sad for the beach community that Gino had graciously hosted for those years.

And Antoine had already dematerialized by then. We had drifted apart when I started spending time in Central America, and after we never had dinner.

I'd heard he got deported. Maybe he didn't have a green card…or maybe there were drugs…. Who knows? The nightlife, the girls, the money, the glamour, the booze. I was never to know, nor to ever see or hear of him again.

But, wherever you are, dear Antoine, you did have your own point of view and helped me with mine. Fighting for peace is still fighting — you have to be peaceful for peace. All hatred is hatred, one brand no kinder than another.

"…And some folks don't hate nothin' at all except hatred."

- sang Bob Dylan

END

OTHER BOOKS BY W. M. RAEBECK

I DID INHALE — MEMOIR OF A HIPPIE CHICK

EXPEDITION COSTA RICA

SOME SWAMIS ARE FAT

SILENCE OF ISLANDS — POEMS

NICARAGUA STORY —
BACK ROADS OF THE CONTRA WAR

TA TA FOR NOW — THE MOVIE

-all books available in print and ebook-
audio on the way

VISIT WendyRaebeck.com to connect